TIGER ON THE TRACK

Bada was standing motionless in the golden grass. The tiger cub looked in the direction of the jeeps, then backed off a little as his brother, Chhota, came staggering out from behind a rock.

'Oh!' Mandy cried, putting her hand to her mouth. 'Look how thin and wobbly he is. Thank goodness we came.'

'Don't raise your hopes too much, Mandy. We don't know what's wrong with him yet,' Adam Hope said cautiously.

Roshan tapped his fingers softly on the steering wheel. 'None of this adds up. We know Tara left her cubs to go hunting and that she made a kill last night. So where is she? She should be here with her cubs now.'

Adam Hope looked at Mandy, who hadn't taken her eyes off the cub. 'Even if Tara was here with Chhota, there's nothing she could do for him. There may be nothing we can do for him either. But we will try.'

Chhota came tottering out towards Bada. The effort seemed to be too much for him and he collapsed on the ground. His body twitched for a few seconds and then was still. Mandy was horrified. To lose him now would be awful.

Animal Ark series

LUCY DANIELS

Tiger
— on the —
Track

Illustrations by Ann Baum

*Hodder
Children's
Books*

a division of Hodder Headline plc

Special thanks to Tanis Jordan.
Thanks also C. J. Hall, B.Vet.Med., M.R.C.V.S., for reviewing the
veterinary information contained in this book.

Text copyright © 1999 Ben M. Baglio
Created by Ben M. Baglio, London W12 7QY
Illustrations copyright © 1999 Ann Baum

First published in Great Britain in 1999
by Hodder Children's Books

A Catalogue record for this book is available from the British Library

ISBN 0 340 72404 8

Typeset by Avon Dataset Ltd, Bidford-on-Avon, Warks

Printed and bound in Great Britain by
Clays Ltd, St Ives plc

Hodder Children's Books
a division of Hodder Headline plc
338 Euston Road
London NW1 3BH

One

'Mandy, James, over here!' Emily Hope pushed through the crowds of people waiting at Jabalpur airport in northern India.

Mandy Hope hurried over to give her mother a big hug as she and her best friend James Hunter emerged into the arrivals area. She hadn't seen her mother for weeks and weeks.

'How was your flight?' Emily Hope asked as she turned to welcome James too.

'Great!'

Mandy and James grinned at each other. They had flown unaccompanied and it had been exciting. The stewardesses had brought them dishes of spicy Indian food followed by delicious sweets that tasted like condensed milk. And at dawn the captain had invited them into the cockpit to see the sun rise over India.

'Dad sends his love and says don't work too hard,' Mandy said, grinning, as they walked to the car park. Her mother laughed. She had already told them that she'd been on call for almost twenty-four hours a day since she'd arrived at the Tiger Reserve in the Shere Khan National Park. There had hardly been time to drive into the neighbouring town of Kasatni to phone home.

Mandy's parents were vets and ran a practice in the Yorkshire village of Welford. But, for the last few months, Emily Hope had been working with an international conservation organisation. During the previous school holidays Mandy and James and Mandy's father, Adam Hope, had visited Mrs Hope in China where she had been working with pandas. Now it was holiday time again, and they were here in India, where Mrs Hope was working with Bengal tigers!

'How's Animal Ark managing without me?' Emily Hope asked, as she led them to a jeep with a tiger's head logo painted on the door.

'Well, Dad said to tell you it's a breeze,' Mandy replied, trying to keep a straight face. She threw her rucksack into the back of the jeep.

James joined in. 'That's right. I heard him saying he could manage with one hand tied behind his back.' Then they both burst out laughing at the indignant look on Mrs Hope's face.

'Seriously, it's been really busy,' Mandy told her. 'Simon was away last week so Dad had to manage without a nurse, and then Jean wasn't well for two days so Gran helped out on Reception. But Simon is back now and Alistair is taking over on Friday so Dad's booked his flight for Sunday.'

Alistair King was a locum vet who often looked after Animal Ark when the Hopes were away. He was taking over so Adam Hope could join them for a holiday.

'Good,' Mrs Hope replied. 'He can rest and relax when he arrives. He must be worn out. Mind you, so am I!' She started the engine and drove out of the car park. 'It's about sixty kilometres to Shere Khan,' she told them.

'So tell us about the park, Mum,' Mandy said. 'How many tigers are there?'

'Well, for a start it's not a park as we know parks. It's enormous!' her mother replied. 'There are still parts I haven't visited yet. It's a whole area made up of hills and valleys, lakes and rivers, meadows and forests, and in a way that's the problem. There are so many places for tigers to roam that they haven't enough staff to keep track of them. Look!' Emily Hope slowed down and drove carefully past a line of boys aged about seven with shaven heads and long flowing orange robes. 'They're trainee monks,' she explained.

When they were safely past, Mrs Hope picked up speed and continued. 'As I was saying, there are places where tigers regularly visit and we are measuring the pug marks – that's the paw prints – of the tigers. You can tell from the size whether it's from a male, female or a young one, and get some idea of how many live there.'

'Will we be able to walk around in the park?' James asked.

'Strictly speaking, no,' Mrs Hope replied. 'Not just anywhere you like. There are paths where it is safe to walk, but there aren't any roads, so we travel by jeep on rough tracks. Or on elephants.'

'Wow!' said James. 'Can you get really close to the tigers?'

'Strangely enough, tigers don't take a lot of notice of people when they're on the back of an elephant,' Mrs Hope said. 'They seem to think that you're part of the animal and you can get very close indeed.'

'Don't tigers attack elephants then?' James asked.

'Not usually,' replied Mrs Hope. 'Elephants are too big and powerful to be a source of food for a tiger. In fact, a healthy adult elephant isn't in danger from any other wild animal.'

The road through the valley was flat and ran alongside a railway line. At a place where the track crossed the road they waited as a train passed. Mandy and James hung out of the windows watching as it chugged by. It was crammed full of people, not just inside where it was standing room only, but also outside, with men, women and children sitting on the roof and standing on the footplates. Some of those on the roof were eating and drinking as if they were having a picnic.

'Can you imagine being allowed to do that in England?' James asked as the train rumbled by.

'No, but it looks like fun,' Mandy joked. 'What happens when they come to a tunnel?'

'That's a point,' Mrs Hope said. 'I haven't travelled on a train here but I suppose there must be tunnels.' She drove across the railway track and on through the valley.

'Have you seen the new tiger cubs recently?' Mandy quizzed. Soon after her mother had arrived at the reserve, a few weeks ago, she'd written to say that the tiger breeding season had begun and that she was observing a newborn litter of four cubs. Mandy was so excited. She could hardly believe that she was going to see real live tiger cubs, out in the wild.

Mrs Hope smiled and nodded. 'I saw them yesterday,' she replied. 'They're so sweet! But I'll have to keep my eye on them,' she added seriously. 'Sasha, their mother, hadn't been back to feed them the day before. I'm told it's not like Sasha to leave her cubs for so long. This is her third litter, and she's usually a good mother ... Whoops!' Mrs Hope put her foot on the brake and waited while villagers moved a cow that had been sleeping in the middle of the road. 'I'm hoping that Sasha will have turned up by now,' she continued. 'The cubs are still suckling, and need their mother's milk.'

'Mm,' agreed Mandy. 'Let's hope so. When will we see them?'

Mrs Hope grinned. 'Well, you might get to see them tomorrow. Billy Biswas, the director of the park, thought you might like to go out on an elephant. That's if you're not too jet-lagged.'

'Wow! We're not a bit tired, are we, Mandy?' said James. 'That would be fantastic!'

Mandy nodded enthusiastically. 'And how are the other cubs you told us about? The two brothers?' she asked. Her mother had also written about the antics of two older cubs, born late last season. They were now eight months old.

Mrs Hope's face grew serious. 'I'm monitoring one of the cubs quite carefully,' she replied.

'Unlike his brother, who is growing strong, the other cub seems to have stopped making progress. There's no injury that I can see, but he's only eating enough to maintain his weight, not to gain any, so he's not growing as he should.'

'Oh dear,' Mandy said, already worried for the cub. 'So what will you do?'

Mrs Hope sighed. 'We might decide to intervene and check him over soon, if he doesn't start to improve by himself.'

They drove on past rice paddies and banana groves, then through a village where dogs barked at them and squawking chickens flew up in the air in alarm. They got stuck behind what looked like an enormous bundle of wood with four legs underneath. The load swayed precariously and took up half of the road.

'What animal is that?' James asked, amazed. 'I can't see its head or body at all.'

'It's an ox,' Mrs Hope replied. 'Carrying firewood.' She sighed. 'Unfortunately, it's probably been gathered illegally from inside the buffer zone. Local people use tremendous amounts for cooking and heating.'

'Heating!' exclaimed Mandy and James together. It was much hotter than the hottest English day.

'Yes, you'll be surprised how cool it gets in the mornings and evenings.'

'What's the buffer zone?' asked James.

'I've read about that,' Mandy cut in. 'It's the forest around a national park, where people aren't supposed to cut firewood or let their animals graze,' she said. 'It acts as a buffer between the park where the wild animals are fully protected, and the villagers who live outside. That's right, Mum, isn't it?'

Mrs Hope nodded. 'But, although the buffer zone was a good idea originally, there are no longer enough park staff to patrol the whole area. The villagers know this and are often tempted to take advantage. It's caused a lot of bad feeling between the villagers and the park staff recently.'

'But don't the villagers want to save the tigers?' asked Mandy, who couldn't imagine anyone not loving these wonderful creatures.

'The people are very poor, Mandy,' Mrs Hope said seriously. 'To them, wood to cook food for their families, and fodder for their animals, is more important than the tigers. If they don't feed their animals properly, they can't sell them at the market – and that's how they make their living. Look, we're nearly there!'

Mrs Hope slowed down, turned off the tarmac road and drove up a winding dirt road that led to a village. She drove very slowly through the village, trying to avoid showering the people with a cloud of dust. Mandy watched a woman who sat in a doorway peeling a pile of green oranges. She nudged James to look.

'Why don't they wait till they're ripe?' he commented.

Emily Hope laughed. 'I thought that too, at first,' she said. 'But I was surprised; they *are* ripe – and deliciously sweet. Apparently, these oranges only go orange in colder climates, here in the tropics they stay green.'

'Why do they call them oranges, then?' James puzzled. 'They should call them greens! Hey, what's that noise?'

A tapping sound grew louder and louder until a herd of goats came streaming out from beside a house on to the dirt road. Skidding and skittering around they bleated wildly as they tried to avoid the jeep. Emily turned off the engine and leaned out of the window. The road around them was completely packed, with not a speck of ground to be seen.

'It's like being in a sea of goats,' Mandy laughed. Just then the goat-herd came alongside the jeep. Clicking and calling to his animals, the man passed by without raising his head.

'He didn't seem very friendly, Mum.'

'Well,' Mrs Hope explained, 'he may have been grazing his herd in the buffer zone and felt worried we might tell him off. Or,' she added lightly, starting the engine and setting off, 'he might simply have been in a hurry. He might be off to market to sell the goats, and that's a whole day's trek away.'

'Does he have to walk all the way?' asked James. 'Couldn't he put them on a lorry?' The idea of walking a herd of goats for a day along the roads in England was unimaginable.

'Lorries cost money, James,' Mrs Hope replied. 'Anyway, it's how they do things in India.'

Now they were through the village and

entering the buffer zone, Mrs Hope told them. There was a lot more forest, but Mandy could see where trees had been cut down for firewood and where the ground and bushes were bare from goats and other domestic animals grazing.

The road began to climb and gradually the forest grew thicker. As they rounded a bend Mandy saw a big carved wooden sign fixed between two ancient mango trees above a metal barrier. 'Welcome to Shere Khan National Park,' Mandy read aloud. 'Isn't that a great name?'

'That's the name of the tiger in *The Jungle Book*,' James remembered.

Emily leaned out of the window, inserted a key into a lock set in a concrete block to raise the barrier and drove through.

'Is that all that keeps people out of the park, and tigers in?' Mandy said, surprised.

'It's more to keep unwanted vehicles out,' Mrs Hope replied. 'People tend not to walk into the park. Tigers, of course, don't know about things like buffer zones and boundaries, but as long as they have a large enough territory and plenty of prey, there's no reason for them to want to leave the park. We rarely see the tigers here, so close to the buffer zone.'

Inside the park the forest was dense on both sides of the track. It was like driving through a tunnel made of great trees, their mighty trunks stretching straight up into a leafy canopy high above. A pair of green parrots with red bills feeding on bright red berries screeched at the jeep as it passed by. Dragonflies hovered above the track, darting away as they approached. Where the sunlight shone through this dense roof of leaves, it dappled the ground with hundreds of little pools of golden light. Mandy realised how hard it would be to see a tiger in the forest. Its stripes would blend in and break up its shape perfectly.

Emily Hope drove slowly up the shady, winding track till suddenly they burst out into the sunshine of a large, well-swept clearing on top of a hill. 'We'll park under the bean tree,' she said, and drove into the shade of a tall tree with big leaves and pods that hung downwards. On one side of the clearing was a long single-storey wooden building with a tin roof. It had a veranda all round with wooden tables and chairs. A sign said LOOKOUT LODGE. On the other side stood a green-painted concrete building. It had a heavy wooden door with a tiger's head logo painted on it.

'That's the hospital block and the offices,' said Emily Hope, as she turned off the engine. The wooden door opened and a man came out. 'And this is Mr Biswas,' she said with a smile. 'He probably knows more about tigers than anybody else in India,' she added quietly.

Billy Biswas locked the door and came across the compound to meet them. Everything about Mr Biswas was big. He was very tall, with broad shoulders and big hands and feet. He wore baggy khaki shorts, a green short-sleeved shirt with the tiger logo embroidered on the pocket, and a wide-brimmed cowboy hat. But it was his smile that Mandy and James noticed most, a big, wide smile that glinted with shiny gold-capped teeth.

'Billy, let me introduce my daughter Mandy and her friend James,' Mrs Hope said.

'Mandy and James, welcome to India.' Mr Biswas made a small bow and shook their hands vigorously. 'It is my pleasure, my pleasure indeed.'

Mandy and James felt both impressed and shy of this big, knowledgeable man.

'You must call me Billy,' he said. 'Everyone does. Now, let's go and have some *chai*, or tea, as you call it,' he said, beaming. He led them over to the lodge where a young girl of about ten and a woman carrying a tray of cups and saucers greeted them. 'Anji, meet Mandy and James. Mandy and James, meet my sister Anji and my niece Sharma.'

Like many of the women Mandy and James had seen at the airport, Anji wore a sari. It was deep-brown shot with gold and orange. *Tiger colours*, thought Mandy. Her thick black hair was wound into a bun at the nape of her neck and dozens of thin silver bangles shimmered on her wrists.

Sharma was dressed in a T-shirt and shorts and her long, glossy black hair reached down to her waist. She was very shy and tried to hide behind her mother, but she couldn't resist peeping out at Mandy and James, lowering her eyelids when they met her gaze.

'Welcome,' Anji said, as she unscrewed the top of an enormous Thermos flask and poured

Billy and Mrs Hope steaming cups of hot tea. 'You prefer a cold drink to tea?' she asked Mandy and James.

They nodded, gratefully. A cold drink was just what they needed.

'Sharma, fetch some *lassi* for these young people here, please,' Anji bid the young girl.

'Oh, I almost forgot,' Emily Hope said. 'I bought a basket of eggs, Anji. I've left them in the jeep.'

'I'll get them,' offered James, and he ran across to the jeep.

'There must be nearly forty eggs here,' he said, as he carried the heavy basket up the steps to the veranda and carefully set it down on the floor.

'Quick, Anji, lock them away before Mikki gets them,' said Billy.

'Who's Mikki?' Mandy asked. At that moment there was a flash of greyish-brown fur as a small animal rushed up to the basket and grabbed an egg. In a second it had run up the wall, on to the roof and over the other side. Billy burst out laughing.

'*That* was Mikki!' Anji said with a smile. 'He's

a mongoose and he loves eggs. You will meet him at breakfast time, so be ready.'

'Is he a pet?' Mandy asked, delighted by this clever creature with a long bushy tail.

'He is a sort of pet, but he has to work for a living,' explained Billy. 'It's Mikki's job to keep the snakes and rats out of the camp.'

Sharma returned with two tall glasses filled with a creamy white liquid and a plate of cartwheel-shaped orange sweets covered with syrup.

'Umm, *jelabis*, my favourites,' said Billy, passing them round. 'I mustn't eat too many of these.' He patted his stomach. 'I need to lose some weight or I will be too heavy for the elephant.'

Mandy and James sipped their *lassi*. The sweet, yoghurty drink was deliciously refreshing.

'What news of Sasha?' asked Mrs Hope. 'Has she returned to her cubs?'

'No, she still hasn't been sighted,' Billy replied, quietly. 'I am worried that something has happened to her. I have sent Roshan with the jeep to check the cubs. Roshan is my head ranger and he's also Anji's husband,' Billy explained to James and Mandy. 'If Sasha *has* disappeared that makes four tigers in three months that we know of. There could be many more. We need to keep up the patrols.'

Billy sighed, picked up his cup and finished his tea. 'I sent Sasha's two older cubs to a reserve that needs breeding females,' Billy told them. 'Two wardens had to accompany them. It's left us very short-staffed, very unprotected if poachers are here.'

'Poachers!' Mandy exclaimed. 'It would be terrible if Sasha can't return to look after her cubs because she's been taken by poachers!' She looked at James. 'We can help to keep guard, can't we, James? It's terrible to kill tigers for their fur.'

'Bengal tigers aren't just hunted for their skins nowadays, Mandy,' Billy explained carefully. 'More and more tigers are being taken for use in Chinese medicine.'

'Tigers as medicine!' James screwed up his nose.

'Chinese medicine uses tiger bones and organs. Almost every part of the tiger is valuable,' Billy continued. 'There is such a demand that they can't keep up the supply. The Balinese, Caspian and Javanese tigers are now extinct, and the Indochinese tiger has almost been wiped out, too. So now the Bengal tiger is in even more danger from poachers.'

'But what do the people who take the medicine think tiger bones do?' asked Mandy.

'Good question,' said her mother. 'There is no proof at all that tiger products have any healing properties. In fact, when a laboratory tested some of the tiger bone tablets, they found poisons had been added to them in very small quantities. It was these poisons causing a reaction that were making people think it was a powerful medicine and nothing to do with the tiger bone. Tigers' bones, like our bones, are mostly made up of calcium.'

Mandy shuddered. 'So the tigers are being killed for nothing. That's horrible.'

The rumble of an engine interrupted their conversation. A jeep drove into the clearing and stopped outside the hospital block. A boy jumped out and waved to them.

'That's Rajiv – Roshan and Anji's son,' Billy said. 'I wonder if Sasha's been back to feed her cubs. Let's go and see.'

Roshan opened the back of the jeep and helped Rajiv lift out a crate covered with a blanket. Gently Billy lifted the corner and peeped inside, then removed the blanket for the rest of them to see. Three small tiger cubs were curled up all over one another in a tangle of big paws and soft, furry heads that seemed too large for their little bodies. Opening their big milky-blue eyes they blinked in the sudden sunshine and stared up at Mandy.

'Oh,' said Mandy, almost lost for words at this

wonderful sight. 'They're gorgeous!' She reached out to the cubs, then stopped and looked at Billy. 'May I?'

Billy nodded.

Mandy put her hand in the crate and picked up a soft furry bundle. The cub was about the size of a domestic cat. It nuzzled her neck, licked her ear, and mewed weakly. Mandy could feel its tummy was quite hollow.

'They are hungry,' Roshan said. 'They had left the den looking for their mother. That's why I had to bring them in.'

'Where's the fourth?' Billy asked softly.

'A leopard killed him,' Rajiv replied gravely.

'Cubs this size are very vulnerable. Their mother has to leave them to hunt and they should stay safely hidden in the den,' Billy explained to Mandy and James. 'In the first few weeks of life, if they venture out, they are in danger from predators like leopards and jackals – even male tigers sometimes kill cubs. Often, out of a litter of three or four, only one will survive. And sometimes none do.'

Mandy felt sad for the poor little cub that hadn't survived. It was a hard life in the wild for baby animals. But these three were safe now.

'I will prepare a feed,' Anji said. 'Come along. Bring them inside out of the hot sun. Tigers don't like to get too hot, you know.'

'They're dehydrated too,' said Mrs Hope, taking over. 'Slightly sunken eyes.' She pulled up the scruffs on the back of their necks. When she released them, they slowly returned to normal. 'We need to get some fluids into them right away.'

Soon, Mandy, James and Sharma were safely seated, each with a hungry tiger cub sucking on a bottle of warm milk.

'Have you fed cubs before?' Mandy asked Sharma.

'Yes.' Sharma smiled shyly. 'Uncle Billy lets me help if I'm home. Normally I go away to school but today is the first day of the holidays.'

Mandy could hardly believe that just yesterday morning she had woken up at her home in Welford. When Gran and Grandad had driven them to the airport it had been drizzling and chilly, and now here she was in the tropical Indian jungle feeding a tiger cub. And tomorrow, she would be riding on an elephant!

India was turning out to be an exciting place.

'I wonder what's happened to their mother?' James said. 'It's awful to think that these cubs could be orphaned because of poachers.'

'And a medicine that doesn't even work!' added Mandy indignantly.

'Uncle Billy says that, in Chinese medicine, people are told that if they eat tablets made from tigers they will become strong like the tiger.' Sharma shrugged. 'I don't know why they believe such a thing.'

The door opened and Billy and Rajiv came in carrying a bale of straw. They made a bed with it on the bottom of one of the four animal cages that lined the walls and Mandy, James and Sharma put the cubs in to sleep.

'What do you think their chances are?' James asked Billy.

'If we can find their mother soon, then quite good. If not . . .' Billy shrugged his shoulders. 'If only the poachers realised that in removing the mothers they are fast removing any future tigers. There are some people, and I try not to think like it myself, who believe that tigers like these little ones here will be the last generation of wild tigers in the world.'

'What! No tigers except in zoos?' Mandy gasped.

'No. Not unless we can find a way to save them, somehow.' Billy smiled sadly.

'That's why your work is so valuable, Billy.' Emily Hope was standing at the door. 'Anji sent me to fetch you all to dinner. We'd better not keep her waiting.'

Two

Lookout Lodge only had room for the few visitors like Emily Hope who were working or studying in the park. A makeshift space had been prepared for Mandy in the stockroom alongside the bottles of cooking oil and bags of flour. James was next door in the library-cum-research room. The walls were lined with shelves of books and piles of papers.

Mandy and James were so tired that they slept well into the morning. It was the sound of a jeep returning that woke them. Mandy dressed and went outside.

'We thought we'd let you sleep; you were obviously very tired,' said her mother. 'Billy and I usually work in the office in the morning and then we tour the reserve in the afternoons. We thought we'd go on the elephant this afternoon. You two can come as well.' She smiled at James who came out of his room yawning.

Anji came along the veranda with some fried eggs and bread for them. 'You could go with Rajiv and help wash Yasmin this morning,' she suggested.

'Yasmin?' queried James.

'Yasmin is the elephant.' Mrs Hope explained. 'That's a good idea. You'll get to know them both.'

After Mandy and James had eaten their late breakfast, Rajiv took them down the path leading to the river. Yasmin was snoozing in the shade. When she heard Rajiv's voice she rolled over on to her knees and stood up. A chain was attached from her front foot to a tree, which Rajiv explained was to stop her going off on her own. Mandy knew that Asian elephants were not quite as big as the elephants they had seen in Africa. Yasmin's ears were much smaller, but standing this close to her she still looked huge.

Rajiv went into a little hut nearby and came out with some green sticks that looked like bamboo. When the elephant saw them she trumpeted loudly.

'Yasmin, meet Mandy and James,' Rajiv introduced them, but Yasmin was after the sticks. 'Wait while I cut it for you.' Rajiv pushed her trunk away. 'This is Yasmin's favourite treat – sugar cane,' he explained.

Mandy and James watched fascinated as Rajiv stripped away the hard outer layer with a sharp knife to reveal the white fleshy fibres inside. He gave a large piece to the elephant who crunched it up immediately, then he handed a smaller piece each to James and Mandy.

'Chew it to get the juice, then throw it away,' Rajiv told them.

Mandy bit hard and released the juice. It tasted like liquid sugar. 'It's fantastic,' she said, working her way along the strip of cane.

Rajiv handed her a piece and motioned for her to give it to Yasmin.

Mandy held it out and Yasmin gently picked

it up with the tip of her trunk and put it in her mouth. 'How old is she?' she asked.

'Yasmin is forty,' Rajiv replied. 'My father had her before me. Since I was small, before I could even walk, my father has been teaching me to be an elephant-keeper, a *mahout*, like him and his father before him. Now that I am fourteen I am able to leave school and work in the park with my father. Elephants cost a lot of money and this park can only afford one, so when the visitors come she works very hard, taking tourists out looking for tigers. Yasmin loves to work, as you will see. But now it's time for her bath.' He went into the hut and returned with a broom.

'What's the broom for?' asked James looking around. There didn't seem to be anywhere to sweep.

'To scrub Yasmin,' announced Rajiv with a grin. 'Want to try?'

James took the broom and felt the bristles. 'Isn't this a bit rough?' he asked as Rajiv led the elephant down the beach into the pebbly shallows.

'No, she loves it,' Rajiv replied. 'Scratch her on the back of the neck with it.'

Soon Mandy and James were taking it in turns to wash the elephant's thick, crinkled skin. It was like corrugated leather. Yasmin certainly did love being brushed; she splashed and squealed, banging the water with her trunk. They stood knee-deep in the river and threw buckets of water over Yasmin while Rajiv stood by her head talking to her in Hindi. Then, on Rajiv's order, she carefully turned her huge body over on to the other side, taking care not to send a tidal wave over Mandy and James who were already soaking wet.

As Mandy scrubbed Yasmin with the broom her worries about poachers drifted away. Maybe it would all come good in the end. Perhaps Sasha would return to her cubs. Perhaps they'd even see her this afternoon. That was something to look forward to.

When the elephant was clean Rajiv tethered her and they all walked slowly back to camp. As they entered the compound the smell of spices drifted in the air. By now their clothes had almost dried in the hot sun and they were starving hungry again. As Emily Hope and

Billy came out of the hospital carrying files and papers, Anji and Sharma began to bring steaming bowls of food to the table.

Mandy and James told the others about Yasmin's bath as they tucked into the spicy dishes of potatoes, green beans and spinach, fluffy orange-flavoured rice and a bowl of dhal made from green lentils.

'After lunch it will be time to feed the cubs again,' Emily told them.

'And time to clean them out,' Billy added.

'I will help you,' Rajiv offered, 'as you helped me to wash Yasmin.'

It was the hottest part of the day, but the hospital was cool. While Mandy, James and Sharma fed the cubs, Rajiv removed all the soiled bedding, thoroughly scrubbed the cage and put fresh straw down.

'These little ones don't make too much mess, with just milk. You can tell a lot from tiger scat, you know.'

'What's tiger scat?' Mandy asked, stroking her cub gently as it slept contentedly on her lap. There was a tiny piece missing from its ear, she noticed.

'Scat is the droppings,' Rajiv answered. 'You can tell what a tiger has eaten, sometimes the fur of a deer, or maybe you find part of a frog. I will show you when we go out,' he told them. 'When we finish here we can go and get Yasmin ready. By the end of today you will know a lot about being a *mahout*!'

Yasmin seemed to know she was going out as soon as she saw them coming down the path. Rajiv got a long cane from the hut and tapped her on the leg. Yasmin knelt down and Mandy helped Rajiv spread thick sacking mats across her to protect her big lumpy backbone. Then James helped him to lift on a wooden construction that looked like an upturned table.

'This is called a *howdah*,' Rajiv explained, pulling a thick rope under the elephant's body and tying it securely on the other side. From the hut he then brought a loop of rope, slipped it under Yasmin's tail and tied it on the back of the howdah. He undid the chain from the tree, draped it over her neck and she was ready to go.

'Is the *howdah* very heavy for her when it's full of people?' Mandy asked.

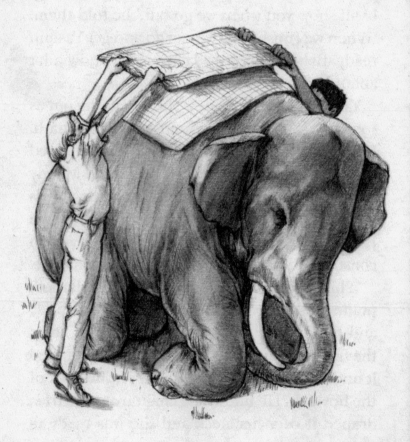

Rajiv smiled. 'It is nothing for her. It is like carrying a little rucksack on her back. Climb up, you will enjoy the ride.'

Mandy took hold of the *howdah* and climbed up the elephant's side until she could haul herself into it. Then she put her hand out and helped James to climb in. There was nothing to hold on to but the wooden legs.

'I will take her to the river for a drink before we go,' Rajiv said.

As the elephant carefully stepped down the sloping bank, the *howdah* titled precariously to one side. Mandy rolled her eyes at James and clung on tight, feeling sure they were going to slide off.

Rajiv laughed at their startled faces. 'Don't worry, Yasmin is teasing you.'

When the elephant had drunk enough Rajiv tapped her trunk lightly with the stick. She stretched it out and Rajiv climbed up and sat on her neck. He paddled her head with his bare feet but Yasmin wasn't ready to move. She put her trunk in the river, sucked up a load of water, then sprayed it all over herself and her passengers to cool them down.

'What a strange feeling,' Mandy said, as they swayed along, up the track towards the camp. Brightly coloured butterflies fluttered by their heads.

'Elephants walk very slowly,' observed James.

'Better to see things, James,' said Rajiv. 'But elephants can run very fast too.'

When they reached the camp Rajiv climbed down and led Yasmin to a set of mounting steps fixed to a tree, where Emily Hope and Billy Biswas were waiting.

'I had better sit at the back over her tail to balance the weight properly,' Billy said, as he climbed up the steps. Mandy felt the *howdah* sway as Billy pulled himself in. With Emily Hope in the front and Mandy and James in the middle, Rajiv settled himself on Yasmin's neck.

'You'll still need caps, you two,' said Emily to Mandy and James, as she pulled on a straw hat with a wide brim, and passed two baseball caps over to them. 'Even this late in the afternoon the sun is still very fierce. You don't want to burn on your first day.'

Mandy and James put on the caps, which had

the same tiger motif on them as they'd seen around the camp.

Billy wore a cowboy hat that he said a real cowboy had sent him from America and Rajiv had already wound a strip of cloth around his head to make a turban.

The narrow forest track twisted and turned so much that they lost all sense of direction. Eventually they emerged beside a lake. Mandy gasped. Thousands of birds had settled on the water and the surrounding shore: herons and spoonbills, ducks and geese, as well as elegant red-headed cranes. On the far shore stood a herd of deer, watchful and alert, their coats rich brown with bright white spots.

'What are they?' asked Mandy.

'They are chital deer,' Billy replied.

'Aren't they beautiful?' Mandy observed.

'We have sambar deer here, too,' Billy added. 'They're quite a size – a metre and a half high at the shoulder. Chital deer are smaller – about a metre high, as you can see. And then we have the little muntjac deer, which are only about half a metre high. I believe you have muntjac in English forests.'

'Yes, we do,' Emily Hope said. 'Lots.'

Rajiv moved Yasmin on along the lakeside then turned left into the forest on a rough track. They travelled a short distance, then turned again to enter a small clearing.

'Look,' said Billy, indicating with his hand. Rising through the trees stood a wooden construction, securely lashed together with ropes. At the very top was a square platform with walls made from plaited palm fronds.

'It's a hide,' said James, surprised. 'Who built it?'

'I did,' said Billy. 'I wanted somewhere where I could watch what was happening on the lake and in the forest. From the top you have a view over the whole area. Sometimes I stay all night watching tigers come and go. Once inside, you can't be seen.'

'I suppose if it's a hide we weren't meant to see it, were we?' observed Mandy.

'You are right, Mandy,' Billy answered. 'Many people come here and never find the lake or see the hide. Tourists who will make too much noise and do not truly care for the tiger we take to other places. Here at dawn and sunset you will see tiger.'

Mandy was glad that Billy had chosen to show them the lake and the hide. She looked at James and, when he smiled back, she knew he was thinking the same thing. Wouldn't it be great if they could come here at sunset and stay all night watching tigers until dawn?

The sun was sinking as they followed a creek through the forest. Rajiv halted the elephant.

'Why have we stopped?' asked Mandy.

Billy indicated a patch of leaves on the sandy earth. 'Rajiv has spotted something. Perhaps it is important. He will check.'

Mandy peered down. It looked like a perfectly normal bunch of leaves. Rajiv climbed down Yasmin's trunk, walked a few paces forward, then knelt down to examine the earth.

'It doesn't look like anything much to me,' said James, gazing down at the patch of ground.

'Wait and see,' said Emily Hope. 'You may get quite a surprise.'

Rajiv called up to Billy, nodding his head. 'Tiger passed by this afternoon.'

Mandy gasped. 'That's amazing,' she said. 'How did he know?'

James stared intently down. 'What can Rajiv see?' he asked Billy.

'Let's all look,' Billy said. Rajiv ordered Yasmin to kneel, and one by one they climbed down. Rajiv brushed away the leaves a little more, and there, clearly visible in the sandy soil, was a huge paw print.

'Wow!' said James, taking off his cap and kneeling down to look. 'And you saw this from the elephant's back?'

Rajiv smiled. 'It is easy to see when you know what to look for.' He walked a little further on. 'Look, here is another one. Two back feet . . . and here the front feet. A big female,' he concluded.

'A good tracker can tell a lot from tiger's pug marks,' explained Billy. 'This pug mark tells me she was walking, not running. It looks to me as if she was making her way back to her den before she started her night's hunting.' He looked at the sun. 'We've just got time to take a look if we're quick, Raj.'

When they were all back in their seats James suddenly cried, 'Oh no, I've left my cap. Shall I climb down to get it?'

'Don't worry,' said Rajiv. He called an order in Hindi to Yasmin, who stepped sideways, daintily picked up James's cap with the tip of her trunk and passed it up to Rajiv. Mandy and James laughed with delight.

'Yasmin is a very obedient elephant,' Rajiv said proudly. 'And she is clever, too. When she was being trained my father said she was always the first to learn. She is always willing to try anything.' He smiled. 'When elephants are training they wear a bell around their necks so the *mahouts* can hear them at night. But Yasmin filled her bell with mud so it wouldn't ring and she raided a banana plantation.'

'Is there anything your elephant won't do?' asked James grinning.

Rajiv looked serious for a moment. 'Yes, she won't run downhill. Elephants don't like to run downhill – they fear they will fall.'

'So now you know what to do if an elephant charges you: run down, not up, a hill!' said Billy, laughing. 'Meanwhile, we've got a tiger to find, Rajiv, so let's go. Hold tight, everyone.'

Mandy felt a thrill of pure excitement. She really was here, looking for tigers in the wild!

They all clung to the wooden poles as Rajiv paddled Yasmin's head with his bare feet. The elephant moved forward with a lurch and when he tapped her head with his stick she broke into a gentle run. She crashed through the elephant grass that was taller than a man and clambered up and along a hillside covered with huge clumps of bamboo. Mandy felt scared and exhilarated at the same time, especially when the *howdah* slipped slightly to the left and she thought she might fall out. Her knuckles were white from holding on so tightly. Every so often Rajiv would halt her and check the ground. When finally they reached a forest of tall trees, Mandy felt quite glad that the elephant was walking slowly again.

'I'm very glad elephants don't run downhill,' said Emily Hope, turning a relieved face to Mandy and James.

'I feel seasick,' said James.

Under the trees it was cool and the last rays of sun made the forest floor glow with dappled sunlight.

'This is called a sal forest,' said Mrs Hope. 'The wood of these trees is similar to teak, and they are deciduous.'

'So they drop their leaves every year,' said James.

Mrs Hope nodded. 'There's a huge variety of forests in India because it's a vast subcontinent. In this reserve alone there are grasslands, bamboo forests, several kinds of hardwood forests, and every area is preferred by different kinds of animals and birds.'

In the distance they heard a deep bark, repeated several times.

'Sambar,' said Billy. 'One of the big deer – and it's barking a warning. That means there could be a tiger nearby. Listen.' A chattering sound grew closer and suddenly a troop of monkeys ran along a branch of a nearby tree, long tails flying in alarm. 'Langur monkeys,' Billy continued. 'Another clue. A scout monkey watches out for predators and warns the whole group,' he explained quietly. 'Try to keep your voices low and no sudden movements.'

Rajiv nudged the elephant gently forward towards some huge boulders overgrown with tree roots and ferns.

'Look, Mandy and James.' Billy pointed to a

pool of sunshine on the forest floor about thirty metres away.

'What?' Mandy whispered, craning her neck forward and squeezing her eyes together trying to see.

'Over there, by the fallen tree, near the rocks on the right,' prompted Billy.

'Ah, yes,' breathed Emily.

'But all I can see is a bush with orange flowers and a . . . oh!' Mandy held her breath in wonder. As she watched, the orange flowers seemed to come alive and take shape. And then the shape became a whole and Mandy could see it clearly.

A tiger.

Gracefully it padded towards the boulders, looking straight at them. Mandy thought even the tiger would hear her heart thumping. She could hardly believe it was happening, but it was. She was in India, on an elephant and there, in front of her, was a tiger, her very first tiger in the wild. Suddenly, as if to prove it, the tiger gave a deafening roar that made them all jump, then stood up on its hind legs and scraped its front claws down the trunk of a tree over and over again. It was a terrifying display of power and strength. Mandy shivered with excitement.

'That's a scratching tree. She's marking her territory,' Billy said in a low voice. 'Tigers have scent glands in their paws.'

Keeping an eye on the elephant, the tiger padded towards the rocks, lay down and watched them. For Mandy it was a magic moment. 'I don't think I've ever seen such a beautiful creature,' she said.

James nodded slowly. 'Look at the power in those muscles!'

'We'll just wait a few moments,' Billy said. 'We know this tigress. We call her Tara. Watch the rocks above her.'

Mandy saw it first: a cub, but not a tiny one like those they had fed earlier. This one was quite big, about half a metre high. It climbed down the rocks and nuzzled its mother, who didn't want to play and pushed it away with her paw. The cub then padded over to the fallen tree and scratched the bark, copying the actions of its mother. Then it was distracted by a dragonfly, which it chased, trying to catch it with its big, clumsy paws. They were all so engrossed watching the scene that none of them noticed a second cub appear, except Billy, who drew their attention to it. The second cub was much smaller than the first and a little wobbly on its legs.

'These are the eight-month-old male cubs I told you about,' Emily Hope said, quietly, to Mandy and James. 'Billy has been watching them since they were born.'

The biggest cub ran back to his mother, knocking the smaller cub over. Gamely the little one got up and tried to play with his brother, but he just didn't seem to have the strength. The big one was so boisterous that the little one didn't stand a chance.

'The difference between them is much more noticeable than when I watched them last,' Billy said gravely. 'The smaller one has definitely weakened.'

'What do you think is wrong?' James asked.

'It could be many things,' Billy replied. 'It could be genetic: that means a problem the cub has been born with.' Emily Hope nodded in agreement. 'Or it could be that the mother is favouring the bigger cub,' Billy continued. 'But somehow I don't think so. I watched her share a kill with them once, and while she let the bigger cub help himself, she tried to help the little fellow to eat. And once, I saw her bring him a mouse, as if to encourage him. We've named the strong one Bada, which is Hindi for big, and the little one Chhota.'

'That means small,' added Rajiv.

Mandy turned to her mother. 'Could he have a bad tooth, Mum?'

'I'd have to examine him to find out, Mandy, and that's not always wise.' Mrs Hope looked at Billy, who was frowning.

'We have to be very careful, Mandy, before we remove a cub from its mother for any reason,' Billy replied. 'She may not accept it back, and then it would be much worse off. Tigers learn everything from their mothers in the first year or two of life. I don't want to interrupt that.' He watched the tigress. The two cubs were climbing all over her. 'Tigers have to be physically perfect. If a tiger has a defect of any sort, it puts it at such a disadvantage that it probably wouldn't be able to live in the wild.' Billy took a notebook from his top pocket and wrote something down. 'I know it's hard but perhaps this little one isn't meant to survive.'

'But surely . . .' Mandy began, then stopped as her mother shot her a look that said, *Don't argue with the experts!*

But Billy noticed that Mandy was upset. 'We will keep an eye on him, Mandy,' he told her. 'I will make a decision in a few days. But now we must go back. You have cubs to feed before you sleep!'

Back at camp, Mandy and James climbed down from Yasmin and raced across the compound to see the cubs.

'Look!' Mandy said triumphantly. 'He knows me already.' She opened the cage and the cub with the piece missing from his ear came straight out into her arms. 'Here comes dinner!' Mandy said as Sharma came in with the feeds.

'Whoa, slow down.' James was trying to pick up his cub but it got so excited at the sight of the bottle that it knocked the other one over and kept trying to get between the bars of the cage.

'You just want to sleep all the time, don't you?' said Sharma, as she picked up the last cub. Soon all they could hear was a contented slurping.

When they had finished feeding, Mandy wiped the milk from round the cubs' mouths to stop them from getting sore. Sharma's cub hung over her shoulder sound asleep. Mandy could feel her cub's little tummy was round and full and his eyes were closing. Even James's boisterous cub sat yawning and stretching on his lap.

'How will they manage if their mother doesn't return for them?' Mandy said, worriedly. 'Who will teach them the things they need to know?'

'Uncle Billy cannot keep them until they are old enough to manage on their own,' Sharma told them. 'He can't teach them to hunt. Only their mother can do that. He hates it, but he may have to send them to a zoo.'

'But that would be awful!' cried Mandy. 'There must be a way for them to go back to the wild.'

'The only way to help them do that is to find out what's happened to their mother,' Sharma said.

Three

Early the following morning Mandy stood on the veranda, her fleece zipped up against the chilly air. As she looked down over the treetops, the sun was just beginning to rise and the forested valley below was white with morning mist. Everything was still and silent.

'Wild India is beautiful, is it not?' said a soft voice behind her. It was Billy Biswas. Mandy nodded.

'Once it was all like this, and the tiger could roam where it wanted,' Billy continued. 'Now, there are only little pockets of safety here and there over India, little havens where the tiger has a home.'

They watched in silence as the sun's rays reached the tops of the trees and the mist began to disappear. Behind them doors were opening and closing as the camp came to life. Mandy turned and smiled at Billy. She liked this big, kind man.

The door to James's room opened. When he saw Mandy he beckoned her in. The walls around his makeshift bed were covered in books.

'Look, Mandy, some of these books are really old. Look at this.' James held the book up for Mandy to see.

Mandy wrinkled her nose in disgust. It was a picture of a man standing in front of a wall covered with tiger skins.

'This man claims to have killed more than a thousand tigers, years ago,' said James. He gave Billy, who was standing in the doorway, a horrified look. 'How could he do that?'

'He was not the only man to kill so many tigers, James,' said Billy. 'In those days, a tiger was a trophy. Many maharajas, the lords of old

India, invited guests to tiger shoots, rather like people are invited to a party nowadays. It was considered great fun, great sport.'

James closed the book with the offending photograph.

'Couldn't someone have stopped it?' asked Mandy, her eyes blazing at the thought of all those tigers being shot for fun.

Billy nodded. 'Killing for sport was abolished in 1970 and since then it has been against the law to kill a tiger.' He sighed. 'The tiger could have recovered its numbers – but other threats then came along: people chopped down the tiger's forests to grow food and make firewood. Slowly, the tiger has lost his land to the people.'

'And tigers need the forests to hunt in,' said James.

'That's right,' said Billy. 'There also have to be enough animals in the forest for tigers to eat. But the local people sometimes kill deer for food, which leaves less for the tiger.'

'And then there's the poachers,' Mandy added, angrily.

Billy nodded. 'The fewer tigers there are in the world, the more valuable they become to us – but also to the poachers.'

'How do the poachers work?' asked James.

'They have many ways,' Billy replied. 'Sometimes they use poison, putting up poisoned bait. Other times they set snares. Sometimes . . .' Billy looked from James to Mandy, 'they fix dynamite to the meat and the tiger blows itself up.'

Mandy cringed at the horror of it.

'But often the animal just seems to disappear,' Billy continued. 'We know that live animals are taken to be killed for Chinese medicine. The poachers use drugged meat, or sometimes they are very sophisticated and have tranquilliser guns to knock the tiger out. Then they get the tiger out of the park and keep it tied in a holding cage until they are ready to move. With forged papers they cross the border, and that's it.'

'Why do they want to keep them alive?' asked James.

'Because one crushed bone looks very like another,' Billy explained. 'Some buyers insist on seeing the tiger killed before their very eyes, or they won't pay.'

'That's *horrible*. Do you think that's what

happened to Sasha?' Mandy asked worriedly.

'I don't know, Mandy,' Billy replied. He scratched his head in frustration. 'If the park had more money I could employ more wardens, and mount a full-scale search, in case Sasha is lying somewhere, trapped or injured. I could even send someone into Kasatni to search places where she might have been hidden by poachers. At least then I'd feel I had done everything I could to save Sasha and her cubs . . .'

'Good morning, everyone.' Roshan walked in from the veranda. 'Anji will bring breakfast soon. I am going out on morning patrol.'

Billy handed Roshan a radio handset and the warden walked over to his jeep.

Anji and Sharma came out of the kitchen, Anji carrying breakfast things for the table and Sharma holding bottles of milk for the tiger cubs.

At the same time Emily Hope emerged from her room, tying her long red hair off her face in preparation for the busy day ahead. 'Ah, time to feed the cubs,' she observed, seeing the bottles.

'Come on, James.' Mandy sprang up. 'They get their breakfast, and *then* we get ours.' She laughed at James's pained expression as she ran to take the bottle from a smiling Sharma. 'You're *always* hungry!'

'Ouch! This cub is always hungry too,' James noted a couple of minutes later, as the cub nibbled at his fingers with tiny sharp teeth.

When all three cubs were happily feeding, Mandy said, 'James, I've had an idea.'

'What is it?' he asked, stroking the soft fluffy white fur on the inside of his cub's ear.

Mandy leaned forward, her eyes wide and serious. 'You heard Billy saying that if he had the people to do it, he'd set up a thorough search for Sasha,' she said. 'Well, *we* could try to find her.'

'But how would we know where to look?' James pointed out. 'We don't know our way around Shere Khan or Kasatni.'

Mandy's face fell, then immediately brightened again. 'Perhaps Rajiv would help us,' she said. 'He knows the park well, and,' she looked at Sharma, hopefully, 'he might know Kasatni, too. Does he, Sharma?'

Sharma nodded. 'Yes, very well. He went to school there.'

'And do you think he'd want to help us?' Mandy asked, with bated breath.

Again, Sharma nodded her head.

Mandy looked back at James. 'Then we must try!' she persuaded.

'You're right,' James agreed. 'But how would we get there?' He turned to Sharma. 'I don't suppose there are buses, are there?'

Sharma gave a little laugh. 'A bus comes by the main road once a week. Mostly the people from the village must walk into Kasatni. Uncle Billy occasionally goes to Kasatni on business,' she continued, 'but only when he has to; he prefers to be out here in the jungle among the animals.'

By this time, the cubs had finished their milk. Mandy, James and Sharma went over to the lodge for breakfast.

Billy, Rajiv and Mrs Hope were already seated at the table, helping themselves from a large platter of sliced pineapple, banana, orange and mango.

'This is *naan*,' Anji said to Mandy and James,

as she brought a pile of warm, freshly baked, flat breads to the table. 'And here are boiled eggs,' she said, removing the heavy lid of an earthenware pot. 'But remember to put the lid on, or Mikki will take them.' There was hot sweet tea and fresh coconut milk too.

Mandy tried a slice of mango. The yellow, perfumed flesh was sweet and delicious. 'Mmm, this is really good,' she said.

'It is even better with yoghurt,' Anji said, smiling. 'I'll fetch some.'

She went to the kitchen, but returned almost immediately, looking worried. 'Roshan just called on the radio,' she said to Billy. 'There are some villagers at the gate who want to talk to you. They are very angry. He is bringing them in the jeep.'

All thoughts of breakfast forgotten, everyone waited for the villagers to arrive.

Mandy and James had expected a few people, but when the jeep finally chugged into view they could hardly believe their eyes. The inside was crammed full, two men hung from each door, and four stood on the tailgate at the back. Three more sat on the roof and one was perched on the bonnet, the opposite side to Roshan, who could only just about see through the windscreen. It would have looked comical – except that the men were scowling and they carried long sticks.

The jeep came to a halt and everybody climbed out. Some of the men were wearing traditional *dhotis* – wide strips of white cloth wound around the waists and legs then caught up at the front to form loose trousers. Others wore trousers or shorts, and most had on long-sleeved shirts. Some had rubber flip-flops on their feet; others were barefoot.

Billy stood on the veranda at the top of the steps to greet them. As soon as he'd done so, one of the men came forward as a spokesman for the group and he and Billy began a heated discussion. Occasionally the others shook their fists at Billy and gestured at the forest and parklands, as they listened.

Rajiv translated for Mandy and James. 'The men are saying that several goats have gone missing and they blame the tigers,' he began. 'They say that it is wrong that they were driven off this land in the first place. If they had the parkland back they could grow crops and they would have all the trees in the forest to sell for timber. It is bad enough that tigers take the land; now tigers are taking their goats.' He paused and listened for a moment then gave a little gasp. 'The men say if any more goats are taken they will kill the tigers.'

Mandy was shocked. She looked at James. 'But they can't!' she cried, more loudly than she meant to. 'It's against the law to kill tigers.'

A man in a white shirt and trousers cut off at the knee stepped forward and looked at Mandy.

He spat out in broken English, 'Tiger not care about law. Tiger come outside park. Tiger kill – we kill tiger. End!'

And with that, the men began to move back toward the jeep, muttering among themselves. Billy went after the man who had spoken to Mandy but he shrugged Billy away.

Rajiv turned to Mandy and frowned. 'I am sorry. That man is my Uncle Sunnil.'

Four

'Don't look so worried, Mandy,' said Anji, in an attempt to cheer her up. 'We will sort it out. Sunnil, Roshan's brother-in-law, is angry at the moment, because he has lost some of his animals to a tiger. He will calm down.' But she didn't sound convinced.

'But he was right in a way,' Mandy replied, quietly. 'Tigers don't know laws or boundaries. So how can they know to stay inside the park?'

Anji looked at Billy. He sighed and sat down. 'I can only tell you, Mandy, that, in all my years at this reserve, I have never known a tiger to stray into the buffer zone. The tigers here have enough food and no need to stray. I don't believe the tigers are to blame. Something strange is going on, it doesn't feel right.'

'But just supposing one did stray, would the villagers really kill it?' asked Mandy with a frown, still not completely reassured.

'I don't know, Mandy. I hope it won't come to that. Tigers are wary of people. The only tiger that goes where there are people is an old or injured tiger that cannot hunt.'

'Is that when a tiger becomes a man-eater?' James asked.

'I don't like that name,' Billy said with a grimace. 'Sometimes, very occasionally, when a tiger is old and perhaps has been driven from his territory by a stronger rival, or its teeth are bad and it can't hunt, then it may leave the safety of the park. Mostly it will take livestock, but if it comes across a person it may kill out of hunger or fear. Then it finds that killing people is easy and may try again. But a tiger hunts only for food. Unlike man, the tiger never kills for sport or simply for fun.'

Billy looked out across the park and frowned

as if he was thinking deeply. 'I think that if the villagers believe there is a tiger in the buffer zone then no, they probably won't come anywhere near it.'

'Good,' said Mandy, relieved.

But Billy hadn't finished. 'What they might do instead is put down poisoned bait. I hope that I have convinced them to wait a while and let me sort things out. Take no notice of that fellow's threats. Roshan will calm him down. Sunnil is married to Roshan's sister.'

But Mandy still looked troubled. Emily and Anji exchanged glances.

'Conservation is never easy, Mandy,' Emily said. 'Billy has to take the villagers' feelings on board. They live here too.'

'Don't they realise that saving tigers is *so* important?' Mandy grumbled. 'If they looked after their goats properly the tiger wouldn't be able to take them.'

'This is India, Mandy,' Anji replied matter-of-factly. 'These things are happening all the time, we just have to find a way round them. Every tiger reserve has problems with people; it isn't just here. But Billy is a well-respected man; the

villagers will listen to him. And Roshan will talk
to Sunnil.'

Billy stood up. 'I must get on with my work.
What would you like to do today?' he asked
Mandy and James.

Mandy seized the opportunity. 'We thought
that we could look for Sasha . . .'

Billy raised his eyebrows and glanced
questioningly at Emily Hope.

'That would depend,' Mrs Hope stated firmly,
'on what you had in mind.'

Mandy looked at James, and then at Rajiv.
'We thought that if Rajiv would help us, perhaps
we could search the park, then, if there is no
sign of her, we could search Kasatni – see if we
can find anywhere a tiger might be kept.
Sharma said that Rajiv knew the town well.'

Rajiv nodded. 'I know plenty of likely places,'
he agreed.

'But I gather that Kasatni isn't the safest place
anyway,' responded Mrs Hope, 'and for the
three of you to be running around looking for
stolen tigers seems to be asking for trouble.
People like poachers don't mess around. They
mean business. I wouldn't want you confronting

them. I know you, Mandy!' She raised her eyebrows at her daughter.

Mandy blushed.

Rajiv looked at Mrs Hope. 'I have many friends in town who would help us to look – and keep us safe,' he reassured her.

Emily Hope looked at Billy. 'What do you think?' she asked him.

'I trust Rajiv,' he replied, seriously.

Mrs Hope thought for a moment, then nodded. 'I wondered how long it would be before you two found yourselves a mission for the holiday!' she said, smiling.

'First things first,' said Billy. 'You should start by thoroughly searching the park. Sasha may still be here but unable to get back to her den. Rajiv knows her territory.' He looked at his watch. 'Rajiv needs to see to Yasmin first. If you set off after lunch you should have plenty of time to scout around before it grows dark. I was planning to spend tonight in the hide to watch for her,' Billy mused.

'Is there any reason why they couldn't do that for you too?' Emily Hope asked.

'I don't see why not. Would you be willing

to?' Billy looked at Mandy and James. 'Rajiv has done it many times.'

'Would we?' Mandy said, her eyes gleaming. 'That would be brilliant.'

'You'd better go and pack your rucksacks,' suggested Emily Hope. 'You'll need sleeping bags and insect repellent and don't forget to take your anti-malaria tablets.'

'We'll need our fleeces and water and food for later,' James said.

'Don't forget your binoculars,' Mandy called as he disappeared into his room.

'Torches. And what about a camera?' he called back.

'We can take it this afternoon, but tonight it might be too dark in the hide and the flash could frighten away the animals.' Mandy couldn't wait! 'Wouldn't it be wonderful if we found Sasha? I wonder what we'll see from the hide?'

'I'll take a notebook and pencil,' James added. 'Let's hope we can stay awake all night!'

Mandy went to her room to get her things ready. She was lost in thoughts of looking for Sasha when there was a knock on the door.

Sharma stood there, looking glum. 'I wish I could come too,' she said, near to tears, 'but Mummy said I am too young.'

'But, Sharma,' Mandy replied, 'we need you to look after all the cubs while we're away!'

'Oh! Of course!' Sharma smiled, obviously feeling much better now she had a part to play, too. 'That will take nearly all my time, as I will have to feed them one by one.' Then she added wistfully, 'I do hope that you find their mother.'

Mandy was too excited to eat much lunch but James tucked in as usual. Anji had made them a picnic box of food for later.

Rajiv brought Yasmin up to the compound and they prepared to set off.

'Now be careful and do what Rajiv tells you,' Emily Hope called out.

'We will, Mum, I promise.' Mandy climbed into the *howdah*.

'Call in tonight to let us know how you are,' Billy said, handing Rajiv a two-way radio handset.

Rajiv nodded. 'Don't worry, Yasmin and I will keep them safe. Ready?'

'Ready,' Mandy and James said together, and they were off.

Rajiv urged Yasmin down the path to the river.

The elephant walked downstream for a while. Then Rajiv said, 'Sasha's territory is alongside this stretch of the water.' He tapped Yasmin on the head, and the elephant stepped out of the creek and into the forest. 'If Sasha is still in the park we will find her here. Tigers lie up by day and hunt at night.'

'So she wouldn't go outside her own territory?' James asked.

'Not far,' Rajiv replied.

They searched across the grasslands and up and down the forest-covered hill and thickets of cane. But there was no sign of Sasha.

Then Rajiv said suddenly, 'Look there. See that ledge above those rocks?'

'Where one rock is leaning against another?' asked James.

'That's it. There's a little cave there where the cubs were born,' Rajiv told them.

'Oh!' Mandy exclaimed. 'Is that where you found them yesterday?'

'No. Tigers move their cubs often when they are very small,' Rajiv explained. 'It keeps them safe from predators.' He looked on the ground. 'I don't think she has been near here recently. There are no marks anywhere. See that tree?' He urged Yasmin forward to a tree nearby.

On one side of the tree the bark had been gouged away. 'That's one of Sasha's scratching trees,' he explained. 'She'd also spray it from a scent gland under her tail to mark her territory.' Rajiv leaned across and smelled the tree. 'Very old. I don't think Sasha has been here for a long while.'

Mandy held on to the *howdah* and sniffed at the tree. 'It smells a bit like a cat litter tray,' she said.

'I feel she is not here,' Rajiv said. He slipped down the elephant and walked over to peer inside the den. 'Nothing,' he confirmed.

It was now mid-afternoon. Mandy was feeling very despondent, when Rajiv suddenly put up his hand. They heard a soft cough.

'Monkeys!' Rajiv declared. 'When they cough like that there's a tiger near. Look carefully in the long grass as we pass.'

Yasmin turned to the right and seemed to be deciding the way to go herself. She walked steadily in the direction the noise had come from. They heard the coughing again. Then Yasmin stopped and stood waiting patiently.

Rajiv stared hard into the long grass around them. 'Mandy, James. There!' he exclaimed.

They followed his gaze. Not ten metres away, almost hidden, lay a sleeping tiger.

Mandy's heart leaped. 'Is it Sasha?' she whispered.

Rajiv shook his head. 'No. This is Zemo, the dominant male. He is the father of Sasha's cubs. You want to take some photos?'

'Won't the noise wake him up?' Mandy asked.

'No. Look beside the tree there.' Near the tiger they could see the remains of an animal, covered with leaves. 'Last night's kill. He is sleeping off a big dinner.'

As they watched, two vultures hopped cautiously towards the carcass. Just as they reached it the tiger sprang up and let out a deafening roar, swatting at the birds with its paw. A flurry of feathers flew up as the frightened vultures escaped.

Mandy and James were rigid with shock. Even Rajiv looked a bit nervous. Zemo had clearly not been that deeply asleep! None of them moved as the tiger stood there watching them. Then he lay down again, put his head on his paws and closed his eyes.

Rajiv signalled Yasmin to walk on. 'He is a testy creature, that one,' Rajiv said.

'Why did he react like that to the birds?' James was still a little stunned.

'Nobody steals that tiger's dinner!' Rajiv grinned. 'Nobody!'

The sun was sinking behind the tops of the trees when they arrived at the lake. The late afternoon glow turned a flock of flamingos from pink to gold. Near the water's edge crocodiles basked in the last rays of sunshine before slipping into the water as night cooled the air. Rajiv took the elephant closer.

'Indian marsh crocodiles,' he announced. 'One adult and two young ones.'

A large, powerful-looking crocodile lay half-submerged, its open mouth revealing rows of

pointed yellow teeth, while two smaller reptiles
kept their distance.

Yasmin put her trunk in the lake and took
a long drink. 'Isn't she worried about the
crocodiles?' Mandy asked Rajiv.

'No, she is too big for a crocodile,' he replied.
'It couldn't pull her into the water, so why
should it try? Animals are only interested in
getting something to eat, they don't like to waste
their energy on unnecessary attacks. They
might get badly injured and usually that would
mean death.'

Rajiv turned Yasmin and directed her along
the lakeside towards the track that led to the
hide. A herd of chital deer raised their heads
and watched nervously as they passed by.
They were small, dainty, spotted animals, the
males with antlers that looked too big for their
bodies. A hornbill screeched. Two kingfishers,
brilliantly coloured in iridescent blues and
greens, darted across the track in front of them.
Mandy shivered with a chill of anticipation.

Yasmin turned into the clearing, and there was
the hide. Only now did Mandy notice the ladder.
It was steep and seemed to go up a long way.

'You two go up first,' Rajiv said. 'I will settle
Yasmin for the night.' He climbed down, took
the chain that was connected to the elephant's
front leg and fixed it around a tree.

Mandy stood up in the *howdah* and put on
her rucksack. She reached out for the ladder.
Slowly she began her climb, trying not to think
how much higher she was getting with every
rung, imagining instead the wonderful view
from the top. She felt as if she were climbing
up into the sky. Bravely she persevered until at
last she hauled herself on to the platform at

the top, five metres above the ground, and crawled inside.

It was magic: a little room with letterbox-sized windows cut into the walls all round at different heights.

From her vantage point Mandy had a clear view of the lake. As she watched, a wild boar brought its family of piglets, striped like humbugs, to drink at the edge. She had read that the piglets lost their camouflage stripes at about six months. 'Watch out for the crocodiles,' she wanted to shout, but whispered it instead.

James pulled himself up and looked out at the lake. 'Wow!' he breathed softly. 'We'll be able to see everything that happens.'

Below them Rajiv settled Yasmin for the night. He removed the *howdah* and stored it under the hide with the sacking inside. Throwing his blanket over his shoulder he climbed up the ladder.

'We should sort out our things before it gets too dark,' James suggested.

They got out their sleeping bags to wrap round themselves if it got too cold, put the food

and water in the middle of the floor, and found
their binoculars.

'Look, Mandy,' said James, sitting on the
floor. 'You can even see out from down here.
Billy did a good job building this.'

'It's great,' she agreed. 'But perhaps we
shouldn't talk too much or too loudly. Animals
outside might hear us.'

James peered out through his binoculars. He
nudged Mandy to look. The piglets were racing
up and down the shore, charging into each
other, leaping over a fallen tree and tumbling
head over heels.

'Play fighting, for when they grow up,' Rajiv
laughed softly.

Just then there was a loud grunt and the huge
female thundered down the shore and herded
a tiny piglet that had strayed along the water's
edge. In the lake a dark shape that they had
thought was a log suddenly disappeared below
the surface.

'That was a crocodile,' said James.

'And one lucky piglet,' added Mandy.

'This time at least,' James said, bending to
unpack his rucksack. 'Should we eat before it's

too dark in here to see anything? We don't want to use our torches unless we have to.'

'Good idea,' said Rajiv. He unwrapped a parcel of triangular pastries that Anji had packed for them. 'Mm, my favourite!' he said. 'These are called *samosas*.'

They were filled with spiced vegetables and were delicious. There was fresh fruit to follow, and little sweet cakes that they decided to save for later.

All the while they watched as the night animals came to drink. Far away on the other side of the lake a mist had begun to form.

'Mandy, James! Look by the little rock that sticks out in the water,' whispered Rajiv excitedly. 'Leopard!'

Through their binoculars Mandy and James could make out a leopard, its spots visible in the moonlight as it padded down to the lake, looking right and left. Even when it was lapping the water the leopard was watchful. Fireflies flashed in the trees around them and the hoot of an owl came from somewhere above their heads.

Then came a howl that made Mandy go cold.

'What was that?' she whispered. 'It sounded like a wolf.'

'Jackals,' said Rajiv. They watched, hardly daring to breathe, as a pack of animals the size of large foxes emerged from the forest only ten metres from the hide, and trotted to the lake.

'They must be golden jackals – I read that they're the ones found in India,' said James under his breath.

'That's right, James,' Rajiv confirmed. 'You see the biggest two? They are the parents,' he pointed out. 'The other two who are bigger than the cubs are from the last litter. Offspring don't always leave; they stay behind to help their parents look after the young. Jackals make nice family groups. They look after each other.'

Suddenly the jackals became nervous and hurried the pups away from the lake. Mandy and James glanced at Rajiv, who shrugged. They could see the lake clearly in the moonlight. The night birds were silent and the shore was now deserted.

'Perhaps this is the interval,' joked James.

'Look,' Rajiv pointed. 'Sambar deer. They love to eat waterlilies.' A family of deer made their way to the lake. The male had small antlers for his size compared to the chital deer. Every so often they stopped and stood like statues with only their noses twitching to pick up scents on the wind. They made their way around the lake and waded out to where lilies floated offshore, except for one inquisitive fawn who lagged behind, nibbling in the long grass.

Then everything happened suddenly. A tiger had been lying in wait in the grass beside the fallen tree. The fawn made no sound as the tiger took it down, swiftly and silently. The tiger dragged its kill to the long grass and ate for a few minutes. Then it covered the carcass with leaves and padded away into the forest.

Mandy had been holding herself rigid and now she took a deep breath and let out a long sigh.

'That was a bit of a shock,' James said quietly. 'Did you know it was there, Rajiv?'

'No, James, I didn't,' Rajiv replied. 'But I recognised her.' In the dim light Mandy and James could see Rajiv was smiling. 'It was Tara,' he said. 'I would know her anywhere. She is my favourite tigress.'

'But how did she get there?' Mandy was awestruck by what she had just seen. 'She managed to creep up right in front of our noses and we didn't have any idea she was there.'

'Tigers are very fast but only in short bursts, Mandy,' Rajiv replied. 'Tigers cannot chase their prey very far. Their power is in their stalking. They creep nearer and nearer and they wait . . . And then they pounce!'

'I don't think I'll be going for a walk in the woods tonight,' James joked.

'Uncle Billy says that only about one in twenty hunting attempts is successful,' Rajiv told them. 'Life is hard for a tiger.'

'I suppose that most nights they catch something,' James said, 'or they'd starve.'

Suddenly a terrifying noise sounded out near the hide and echoed through the forest.

'Eeroom!'

'It's Tara,' Rajiv said. 'She is warning other tigers of her presence so that they don't surprise each other.'

Tara was back, and this time she wasn't alone. A cub trotted along behind her. But only one.

Mixed with her excitement, Mandy felt a

worried feeling nagging at her. She recognised the cub as the big, strong one. 'That's Bada, isn't it?' she whispered. 'But where's the other cub, Chhota?'

'I don't know.' Rajiv replied. He sounded a little concerned himself. 'We can check tomorrow.'

'I hope nothing awful has happened to Chhota,' James murmured.

They watched in silence as the tigress shared the meat with her cub. When they had eaten their fill, Tara took Bada back into the forest.

For the next couple of hours absolutely nothing seemed to happen.

They wrapped their sleeping bags round them to ward off the night's chill, and continued to wait.

James took off his glasses and rubbed his eyes.

'Tired?' Mandy asked.

'A bit,' he replied, yawning.

'Why don't we take it in turns?' Mandy suggested. 'I'll watch for a while and wake you if anything comes. Then either of you can take over.'

'OK, but wake us if *anything* happens,' James insisted.

'Yep, don't worry.' Mandy didn't feel the slightest bit tired. She looked out at the lake. It was still. Nothing moved on the shore, and nothing was hiding beside the fallen tree as far as she could make out. Fireflies flashed in the trees and the smell of night flowers drifted in. All was quiet and peaceful . . .

A roar woke them. A roar louder than Mandy or James could ever have imagined. An angry roar, a terrifying roar. And it was very near.

Five

They leaped to their feet and looked out. The roar had stopped but the forest creatures were in panic. Monkeys squealed in fright, shaking the branches of trees as they scampered away. Birds screamed fearfully and they could hear the thudding of hooves as deer galloped off as fast as they could.

'What's happening?' Mandy was too scared to feel guilty about falling asleep. Then there was a snarl, low and threatening, followed by a thud. The hide shook violently.

Rajiv rushed to look. 'It's Zemo! Yasmin is

seeing him off.' Zemo, the big male tiger, had come to investigate and had crept right up to the hide. Even though the elephant was tethered, the tiger was taking no chances. All they saw was the back end of Zemo disappearing into the forest.

Everyone was too excited to fall asleep again. The eastern sky had grown lighter, and soon the sun began to rise over the lake, its warm rays melting the mist.

Despite the exhilarating events of the night before, Mandy, James and Rajiv were gloomy on the ride back to the Lodge, their spirits dampened by the fact that they hadn't found Sasha.

'We'll go and check on Chhota this afternoon,' Rajiv promised.

There was more bad news awaiting them at camp. Several more goats had gone missing and the villagers were extremely angry.

'I just don't believe it,' said Billy. 'There is something very wrong about it all. The tigers have no need to take goats. I'm going down to the river. I need to think.' His shoulders slumped as he walked down the path.

'Poor Billy,' said Emily Hope. 'All his work is falling to bits around him. But I do agree with him. Something smells fishy about all this.'

'Where's Dad?' Rajiv called, as he started Yasmin down the path to the river.

'He's gone with the jeep to collect something in town,' Anji shouted. 'He'll be back shortly. I'll keep breakfast until he and Billy get back.'

Mandy, James and Sharma had fed the cubs and Mrs Hope was checking them over when they heard the jeep.

'I wonder what Roshan had to collect in town that I couldn't have got when I picked you two up?' pondered Mrs Hope as they came out of the hospital.

'Who's that in the passenger seat?' asked James, shielding his eyes with his hand and peering down the track. 'Goodness, it looks like . . .'

'Dad!' yelled Mandy. 'It's Dad!' She raced out to meet the jeep followed by Emily Hope, her red hair flying.

Adam Hope enveloped them both in a huge hug. 'Oh, it's good to see you. It seems ages!' he laughed.

'What a wonderful surprise!' Emily Hope hugged her husband. 'We thought you weren't coming until Sunday. How did you manage it?'

'Well, Alistair arrived a couple of days early. I phoned the travel agent and there was a cancellation on an earlier flight,' Adam Hope told them. 'We faxed the park office in town and they called Billy Biswas. I thought I'd surprise you all, so here I am.'

'You certainly have surprised us – and cheered us all up!' his wife said. 'You're just in time for breakfast. Mandy and James will fill you in on what's been happening since they arrived.'

Adam Hope put his arms round their shoulders as the three of them strolled across the compound. Mandy began telling Adam Hope everything. She almost ran out of breath as they went up the steps to the table on the veranda.

'. . . And we're feeding three cubs whose mother, Sasha, is missing,' Mandy told him. 'We searched for her all day yesterday.'

'And the villagers think the tigers are stealing the goats,' James added.

'And we spent last night in the hide, and—'

Mandy couldn't get the words out quickly enough. There was so much to tell.

'Whoa, you two.' Adam Hope groaned. 'This is all too much for me to take in at once. Let me take a quick shower and then we'll talk.'

Mandy and James showed him to his room and the shower block. A couple of minutes later, they could hear him singing merrily and the splash of water.

'Someone sounds happy!' Billy arrived back as Adam Hope came out of the shower, now comfortable in fresh shorts and shirt after his long journey.

Mandy introduced them and, at last, they all sat down for breakfast.

Adam Hope leaned back to survey the valley below. 'Look at that view. I could sit here all day looking at that.' Mandy sensed he was trying to lighten the mood. He had heard the entire story about Sasha and been told about Chhota.

'Here we are,' said Anji. 'Here are your eggs. Look after them.' She winked at Mandy and James.

Adam Hope put two on a plate and looked quizzically at Anji. 'Look after them?' repeated

Mr Hope. 'Why, what's going to happen to them?'

At that moment something dropped from the roof straight on to him. Mr Hope leaped up in surprise, whooshing the creature off his lap. But Mikki was well-practised at his tricks and, grabbing one of the eggs, he sped away.

'Hey, that's my breakfast!' Adam Hope exclaimed, as Mikki scooted down the veranda and up on to the roof, then sat there eating the egg. Bits of falling eggshell landed in Mr Hope's hair.

Anji and Sharma were giggling and Mandy was laughing too much to speak.

'That was Mikki the mongoose,' James filled him in, trying not to laugh too much at the look of surprise on Mr Hope's face.

'If it wasn't for the fact that he found a cobra under my bed last week, that animal would have to go,' Billy announced.

'That's Mikki's job, Dad,' Mandy told him. 'He keeps the snakes and rats out!'

'Then he should definitely stay,' Adam Hope said, faking a shiver. 'If he keeps the spiders away from me, he's welcome to one of my eggs every morning.'

Mandy, James and Rajiv had fed the cubs and were showing them off to Adam Hope when Billy and Roshan returned from morning patrol in a triumphant mood. 'I knew it!' Billy announced, striding into the hospital block. Anxious to hear what Billy had found, everyone followed.

Billy dumped a plastic bag on the table. In it was the carcass of a dead goat.

'Did you find this in the park, Billy?' asked

Adam Hope. Billy nodded.

'So does this mean the villagers are right, tigers have been killing their goats?' Emily Hope asked, gravely.

Billy shook his head. 'It's an old poachers' trick,' he explained. 'The meat has been left for the tigers to eat. I suspect that it was villagers who left it. It's been poisoned, soaked in insecticide!'

Mandy gasped. Now that it had been pointed out, she noticed a faint chemical smell wafting up from the bag.

Billy turned to Roshan. 'We will go to the village this afternoon, Roshan, and speak with Sunnil.'

Roshan nodded. 'Recently, he's been acting very strangely. He is not himself. My sister is sick. Perhaps the worry is getting him down.'

'There's something else,' Billy continued, frowning. 'I passed by Tara's den and Chhota is very poorly.'

'Oh, no!' Mandy exclaimed. She looked over at Rajiv.

Rajiv nodded. 'That doesn't surprise me.

Chhota wasn't out with Tara and Bada last night,' he explained.

'What can we do? Mum, Dad . . . We must do *something*!' Mandy pleaded.

'That's for Billy to decide, love,' Emily Hope replied quietly. She turned to Billy. 'Do you want to bring him in?'

'I don't want to,' he replied. 'But I do agree now it's probably his only chance. He's fading fast.' Billy put his hands on his hips and stared into the distance, thinking hard.

'Yes. Let's do it. We'll take both jeeps. I'll drive one. Roshan, you drive the other as a back-up.' He strode about giving orders. 'Put a cage in my jeep, Roshan. Emily, if you would come with me. And bring enough tranquillisers for two tigers, please. If Tara is there we will need to sedate her first. Bring enough. She's a big, powerful animal.'

'Could you use some help?' Adam Hope offered.

'We certainly could. Chhota is only about eight months but he'll weigh about forty kilos even if he is thin. We'll need to tranquillise him. Even a little cub like that can do a lot of damage if he's angry or afraid.'

'Looks like I'm having another working holiday!' Mr Hope grinned at his wife.

Emily Hope laughed and kissed her husband's cheek. 'And you wouldn't really want it any other way!' she said.

While Emily Hope sorted out what veterinary equipment she would need, Billy and Roshan carried a cage into the back of the jeep, slotting it between the two back seats.

Mandy, James and Rajiv had been keeping out of the way.

'Do you think they'll let us go?' Mandy asked Rajiv.

Rajiv shrugged. 'Billy is very careful when he's dealing with tigresses with cubs. That's about the only time they won't think twice about attacking. A worker in another park was dragged out of the branches of a tree and mauled by a tigress who thought he was a threat to her cubs.'

'I'd really like to see Billy working in the wild with the tigers,' James said.

Mandy nodded. 'Me too. But it's getting Chhota that I'm worried about. It will be awful if we have to miss everything.'

Emily Hope came out of the hospital carrying her bag.

'Mum, do you think we can come as well?' she asked, trying to sound calm and hide the desperate urge she had to rush straight off to Chhota.

'Mandy, I don't think so. It could be dangerous.' She looked over to the jeeps where Billy and Roshan were sitting ready in the driving seats. Adam Hope was talking to Billy and now he walked over to them.

'I know exactly what you are saying, Mandy. You want to know if you can come along. Well, I'm afraid I asked Billy and,' he shook his head, 'of course Billy's word is final.'

Mandy looked at the ground and scuffed her foot back and forth. 'It's OK, Dad. I understand.' She was desperately disappointed. 'You can tell us all about it.'

'I hadn't quite finished. Billy's final word was yes!' he said, smiling at his wife. 'You can all come.'

Mandy carried on scuffing her foot then suddenly her head jerked up. 'Yes! He said yes!'

Her eyes were ablaze with excitement.

'But he was very specific. On no account are any of you to get out of the jeep at any point. No opening the windows and leaning out. Let's go now. Billy wants you in the jeep with Roshan and me.'

Everyone piled into the jeeps. Unlike the elephant that could go almost anywhere it wanted, Billy and Roshan had to keep the jeeps to the track that led across dried up river-beds, a much longer route to the lake. From there they squeezed the vehicles through tiny spaces where the forest had grown over the track. The engines screamed as they forced them up a steep section where the wheels spun around.

'It's quicker by elephant,' James joked. Eventually they arrived at a spot where they could see Tara's den through the binoculars. It appeared deserted.

James nudged Mandy. 'Look.' He pointed to the boulders where Rajiv had shown them the cubs.

Mandy spotted a slight movement beside then. 'It's Bada,' she breathed.

The cub was standing motionless in the

golden grass. Every so often he walked to the rocks and pushed at something with his paw. He looked in the direction of the jeeps, then backed off a little as Chhota came staggering out from behind a rock.

'Oh!' Mandy cried, putting her hand to her mouth. 'Look how thin and wobbly he is. Thank goodness we came.'

'Don't raise your hopes too much, Mandy. We don't know what's wrong with him yet,' Adam Hope said cautiously.

'If Tara were to return and find someone taking her cub she'd kill them, wouldn't she?' James asked as he watched the cub.

Roshan nodded. 'Without a doubt. To go too close to a tiger's den when she has cubs would be very, very dangerous. Billy wouldn't chance that with a tigress even if he'd known her all her life. If Tara is around Mrs Hope must tranquillise her while we get the cub. Billy doesn't like doing it but that little fellow is on his last legs.'

'If he doesn't die on his own I expect something else would kill him,' Adam Hope looked at Roshan.

'Leopard probably. He is alone and weak.' Roshan tapped his fingers softly on the steering wheel. 'None of this adds up. We know Tara left her cubs to go hunting and that she made a kill last night. So where is she? She should be here with her cubs now.'

Adam Hope looked at Mandy, who hadn't taken her eyes off the cub. 'Even if Tara was here with Chhota, there's nothing she could do for him. There may be nothing we can do for him either. But we will try.'

They watched as, in the other jeep, Emily Hope began loading two dart guns.

'Will Mum have to tranquillise Chhota even though he's so weak?'

Her father looked serious. 'We can't take risks with our own safety, Mandy. We don't want any accidents.'

Chhota came tottering out towards Bada. The effort seemed to be too much for him and he collapsed on the ground. His body twitched for a few seconds and then was still. Mandy was horrified. To lose him now would be awful. 'Is he, has he . . .?' She couldn't finish the question.

'I don't know, Mandy. Billy will wait a while

to be as sure as he can that Tara's not around,'
Roshan advised.

'How does he know she won't come bounding
through the forest just as he reaches Chhota?'
James asked.

Roshan stared straight ahead at the cubs, then
said quietly, 'He doesn't, James.' He indicated
the rifle in the rack above him. 'The bolt is
removed. Only in the worst emergency will Billy
allow me to use it. Only if the tigress takes him
down.'

It was the hottest part of the day. Mandy was
sweating and James's glasses slid down his nose
as fast as he pushed them back. Beads of
perspiration dotted Adam Hope's forehead.
Even Roshan and Rajiv looked hot. In the other
jeep Emily's red hair was damp and springing
into curls with the heat. But none of them
minded the discomfort if the wait meant Billy
would be safe.

At last Billy started the engine. Very, very
slowly he manoeuvred the jeep round so that
Emily Hope was nearest Chhota and had a good
view. Winding down the window she took aim
and fired. Chhota winced as the dart hit home.

Billy waited a few seconds then opened the door. 'Please be ready with the antidote,' they heard him say to Emily.

Billy got out. Slowly he moved towards the cubs. They saw Bada snarl as Billy approached. Billy carried on walking. Mandy's heart jumped as she saw another very slight movement from Chhota. She felt her hands clenching with apprehension as she raised her binoculars to her eyes. As Billy reached Chhota, Mandy thought of Tara. Was the tigress in the bushes, ready to pounce on Billy?

Roshan took the gun in one hand, the bolt in another.

James's fingers were crossed so hard that the knuckles were white.

'Please be all right, please,' Mandy willed repeatedly, in her head. It was a plea both for Billy who was so brave and Chhota who was so weak.

They all let out a collective sigh as Billy reached the cub. Like them Bada watched silently as Billy squatted down, put his arms around Chhota's body and struggled to his feet, taking care to support the cub's head. He could hardly see where he was going as he stepped over the tree roots and waded through the grass. Although Chhota was underweight, he was still heavy and awkward to carry.

By the time he was near the jeep Billy was soaked in sweat, gasping for breath and covered in scratches, but he made it and now Chhota would have a chance. Roshan sprang into action. He ran forward to help Billy with the cub. Adam opened the back of the jeep, prised the bolt from the cage and opened up the front. Together they lifted the cub into the cage, bolted it and leaped back into their seats.

Emily Hope leaned over the back seats and injected the antidote. 'Let's get this animal back to the hospital as quickly as we can.' Billy drove off as fast as was possible on the bumpy ground. Mandy just had time to see her mum give a smile and a thumbs-up as she passed.

Back at the Lodge, Emily and Adam Hope put their expertise into practice.

'First thing is to carry out a thorough examination, before we give him any fluids,' Emily Hope said as they carried the cub into

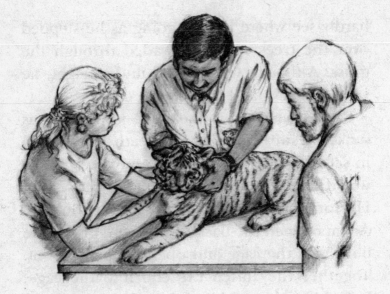

the hospital, 'just in case we need to anaesthetise him.' Adam Hope nodded in agreement.

Within minutes Chhota was laid out on the operating table with Billy holding his head, and the others looking on anxiously.

'Nothing wrong with his jaw or teeth,' Emily Hope reported. 'But he's in a state of collapse. A normal tiger cub of this age wouldn't let us examine it so easily.'

'Pass me that thermometer, please, Mandy,' Adam Hope said.

Mr Hope took the cub's temperature and

checked his pulse. 'Hmm, pulse is steady, if anything a little slow, but then his whole body would slow down because of lack of food. Temperature is slightly up.'

'He flinched when I touched his neck in the jeep,' Billy told them.

'Could there be something wrong with his throat?' Mandy asked.

'That's our next port of call, Mandy,' said her dad. 'A process of elimination. First we'll try for the logical things that can go wrong before we do anything too drastic that might traumatise him.'

'Let me feel your neck, little one,' said Emily Hope. But when she did, Chhota growled and struggled. 'You're not that weak, are you, boy?' she said. 'You've still got a fighting spirit,' Mrs Hope glanced at Billy. 'I think we have no choice but to anaesthetise him and have a proper look.'

Billy nodded. 'Do whatever you need to,' he replied.

Mrs Hope quickly began to snip away a patch of hair above Chhota's paw. 'Could you prepare me some anaesthetic, please, Adam?' she said. 'It's in that cupboard to your left.'

Mr Hope fetched a sterile syringe, unwrapped it and filled it with anaesthetic. After flicking the syringe with his finger to settle the liquid, he handed it to Mrs Hope. She found a vein in the patch of skin she'd prepared and injected it into the cub.

Within seconds Chhota was unconscious.

'We must work fast,' Mrs Hope said, shining a light down the cub's throat. 'It's quite swollen down there, and there's some infection, but I can't see any obstruction. The air passage is clear and so is the throat. Can you pass me some swabs, Mandy? Let's clean it up.'

Mandy's parents worked carefully until the infected tissue had been removed and Chhota's throat thoroughly cleaned.

'Strange thing is, I can't see a wound,' Mrs Hope said. 'there doesn't seem to be any reason for the infection, the skin is smooth and clear.' As she talked she continued to feel all around the inside of Chhota's throat.

'But something must have caused it, Mum!' Mandy said, desperately. They just *had* to find out what was making the cub so weak and ill.

'Wait a minute.' Emily Hope frowned.

'Tweezers someone, quick.' Adam Hope passed over a pair from a nearby tray of instruments.

'Adam, can you hold Chhota's tongue, please?' Mrs Hope said. 'There's something here, I can feel a sharpness.' She began pulling at something. 'That's it, out you come.' She held up a black needle-like spine with a white tip.

'A porcupine's quill!' Billy announced. 'So *that*'s what's been causing all the trouble. I've not seen it myself, but I've heard of cases where a young tiger, not knowing what a porcupine is, has chased one and got a quill stuck in its mouth. It often kills them because they're unable to eat, and the wound becomes infected.'

'But Chhota will be all right now, won't he?' Mandy pleaded.

'Yes, I think we caught him in time,' Emily Hope answered. 'Any longer and the infection could have taken a hold. We won't know until he wakes up.'

Mr Hope had gone back to the drug cupboard and came back with another small bottle. He began filling a syringe. 'This is an antibiotic to clear any infection. The mouth and throat heal very quickly, though he may have a sore throat for a day or two.' He injected Chhota and continued, 'What he *will* need when he wakes up is lots of fluids and some gentle feeding.'

Mandy nodded. 'James and I can help with that.'

'He may not want to swallow solid food,' Emily Hope added. 'But the sooner he does, the quicker he'll build up his strength. Not too much, little and often.'

'No cuddling though,' Billy warned, as he and Adam Hope carried the cub back to his cage and laid him gently inside. 'This cub must stay as wild as possible. Once he gets strong there will be no stopping him. He won't like being cooped up so, whatever you do, don't open the cage.'

Billy took a big water bowl out of the cupboard and gave it to James to fill. 'He'll need fresh water several times a day,' he said. Then he showed them how to release a flap on the front of the cage to enable them to push the bowl in safely. 'Roshan will bring you some deer meat for when Chhota wakes up. Try him with some small pieces – you may have to tempt him.'

'He'll be sleepy for a while when he comes

round,' said Emily Hope. 'Why don't you have lunch and then come back to feed him?'

Mandy stroked Chhota's soft ears through the bars of the cage.

'I think I'd like to wait here to be with him when he wakes up. I'm not very hungry.' She looked at James.

'I can miss lunch too,' he offered. Mandy smiled.

'Go on, you go and eat and then come and help me feed him. There's no point in both of us missing lunch.'

Adam and Emily Hope took off their gowns and went out with the others.

'Come and get us if you're worried,' Mrs Hope said at the door.

Mandy heard their voices getting fainter as they crossed the compound, and then it was quiet. Just the soft sound of Chhota breathing.

'You are going to get well, Chhota,' she told the sleeping cub. 'I know you are.' Mandy smiled as the cub gave a gentle snore.

Six

Chhota was still very weak when he woke up. But his eyes were brighter and his nose cold and damp. Billy showed Mandy how to feed him with marble-sized portions of meat.

'He doesn't want to eat it,' Mandy said, worried that his throat was too sore for him to swallow.

'Once he gets the taste of it he will,' advised Billy. 'You'll have to persevere.'

Mandy tried. She coaxed him with the food but he just lay on his side and looked at her. He wouldn't even lift up his head. Billy had told her not to force him to eat but she couldn't even get him to open his mouth. She was near to tears with frustration when James, Rajiv and Sharma came in to see how she was doing.

'Tigers are tempted by food that fights back. They like to chase it,' Rajiv said. 'I've helped Sharma and James feed the little cubs, so you can concentrate on Chhota,' he added.

'Thanks,' Mandy said gratefully. Rajiv had given her an idea. She ran outside and found a thin length of bamboo. She put the piece of meat on the end and pushed it through the bars behind Chhota's head. Slowly she pushed the meat past his face, wiggling the stick, moving it back and forth. Chhota lifted his head and watched the meat.

Mandy could hardly control her excitement. Rajiv, James and Sharma watched. Suddenly, as Mandy pulled it away, Chhota brought his paw round and snatched at the meat. He sniffed it and, tentatively, began to chew. Then he swallowed, looking a little surprised that he was able to.

'You're no different from a kitten with a ball of wool, are you?' Mandy said, with a huge smile.

When Mandy dangled some more meat in front of Chhota, he grabbed it again. Mandy was delighted.

That night after dinner everyone sat on the veranda discussing Sasha, and what to do next. Reluctantly, Billy had come to the conclusion that it was likely she had been captured by poachers and taken into Kasatni.

Mandy looked at Rajiv. 'We could start our search of the town tomorrow,' she suggested. 'The sooner we go, the more chance there will be of finding her.'

Rajiv nodded enthusiastically.

'Ahem . . .' Adam Hope interrupted. 'Actually, I'm not sure that this is a good idea, after all.' He looked over at his wife. 'Your mother has been filling me in on your plans, Mandy,' he said.

'But, Mum, Dad,' Mandy argued, her heart sinking, 'Rajiv knows the town, and he has friends there who would help us. We'd be really careful. We wouldn't do anything risky. Please!' she pleaded.

Adam Hope looked at his wife.

'If we say yes,' Mrs Hope began. She put up her hand and Mandy, who had leaped excitedly out of her seat, sat down again. 'Just wait and hear me out. If we say yes, I want a promise that if you find anything of importance you won't try to tackle it alone. You will come back and tell us and we'll all decide what to do.'

'And stay with Rajiv,' Adam Hope added. 'We don't want you getting lost in Kasatni. The last thing I want to do on my holiday is spend it in a noisy town looking for you. I'm here for some peace and quiet and a chance to ride on an elephant.'

'Wait till you meet Yasmin, Dad,' Mandy said. 'You'll love her.'

'She's such a clever elephant,' James told him.

'Don't change the subject, you two,' Emily said sternly. 'A promise, Mandy?'

'OK, a promise. I won't do anything silly.'

'Or dangerous,' added Mr Hope.

'Or dangerous,' Mandy finished.

'Me too,' agreed James.

'Then you can go,' Emily Hope said.

'Thanks, Mum, thanks, Dad.' Mandy jumped up and hugged them, then gave a thumbs-up sign to James and Rajiv, who were beaming, too.

'Now we have only one problem,' Rajiv said. Everyone looked at him. 'The bus into Kasatni does not pass nearby until the day after tomorrow.'

'Oh,' said Mandy and James together, as their faces fell in disappointment.

'As it happens, 'Billy said smiling, 'I have to travel to town on business one day this week. I can go tomorrow, and drop you off.'

'Thanks, that would be brilliant!' Mandy replied. 'Problem solved.'

'We'll leave at six. That will give you the whole day,' Billy continued. He looked at Mandy, James and Rajiv. 'I appreciate your help,' he said in a low voice. 'Now, I am off to finish my paperwork. Goodnight, everyone.'

In bed that night, Mandy couldn't stop thinking about tigers. What would happen to Chhota and Bada? Would poachers come for them too, one day? She decided that, not only did they have to find Sasha, they had to find the poachers and stop them once and for all.

'Time to get up, Mandy and James,' called

Adam Hope. 'Are you awake?'

It was the following morning, but so early it was still pitch dark. For a moment Mandy couldn't remember what was happening.

'I'm awake,' called out James. 'Is it six o'clock already?'

'Nearly,' Adam Hope whispered. 'Anji has left a Thermos of tea and some bread for your breakfast. I got up to make sure you were awake. Don't keep Billy waiting. And don't forget you promised you'd be careful.'

'We will,' said Mandy, flinging on her T-shirt and trousers and emerging from the store-room.

'Honestly, we won't do anything silly,' James added, cleaning his glasses on his T-shirt.

'Perhaps I should come with you,' Mr Hope said.

'It's your holiday, Dad,' Mandy replied. 'You sit and enjoy the view, and if we need you, we'll call – promise. So don't worry.'

'But I *will* worry. I'm your father. That's my job!' Adam Hope smiled.

Rajiv arrived and poured himself a cup of *chai*. 'They will be safe with me, Mr Hope.'

'Well, good luck. I'm going to catch another hour's sleep,' Mr Hope said, padding back to bed.

Mandy poured cups of hot sweet tea and they munched on the bread and waited for Billy.

James had just helped himself to another piece when there was a soft thud of a door shutting and Billy came across from the hospital block. 'All ready?' he asked, unlocking the jeep.

'Yup,' said James, putting on his cap.

'Yup,' said Mandy, zipping up her fleece.

Rajiv loaded the jeep as Billy checked his list. 'Right. That's the wheel that needs a new tyre, three empty rice drums, two drums for lentils; we need some more formula mix for the cubs – I can pick that up at the office. What else did Anji ask me to get? Ah yes, the latest film magazine. OK, let's go.'

They drove out of the park in darkness, through the buffer zone and onwards into the village. Cockerels crowed and barking dogs chased the jeep. Once through the village Billy picked up speed. They drove up a steep winding road over a hill, then down into the misty valley. When the road flattened out they could see the distant glow of Kasatni on the horizon.

It was just getting light when they arrived and Mandy's first impression of the town was that it was full to the brim with people, and so busy and noisy it made her feel dizzy. Everybody seemed intent on getting in to the town centre. Vans and buses, lorries, horse-drawn trucks, bullock carts and rickshaws pulled by men were all trying to squeeze into lines of traffic that were jammed to a standstill. And everyone was tooting their horns.

Along the side of the road was a shanty town, the walls of the houses made from tin cans opened out and flattened, with sheets of plastic for roofs. Lots of people were buying food from stalls along the roadside. Outside one house was a stall where small children crowded round a woman selling biscuits and small cakes from big sweet jars. Several other stalls sold freshly peeled oranges piled into pyramids. There were tiny shops, just holes in the walls, where people were queuing. Further along, the jeep passed rows of stalls and kiosks with steaming urns and sizzling pans.

'What are they selling here?' Mandy asked Billy.

'The urns are full of *chai*, tea like you drank this morning. They drink it in little earthenware cups, called *chattis*. They don't return them, just break them on the ground. Here they are cooking delicious foods, *samosas* and spicy deep-fried vegetables. Over there,' he gestured to where a man was stirring a big metal pot with a wooden ladle over a fire, 'he is roasting peanuts in their shells. The pot has sand in it and he stirs it so they all get cooked the same.'

When they reached a traffic light he called out something to a boy who sped off and returned minutes later with a paper cone full of the orange cartwheel-shaped sweets called *jelabis*. Billy dropped a few rupees into his hand and passed the sweets to Mandy and James.

The *jelabis* were dripping with syrup, and delicious.

'Umm, thanks, these are lovely!' James said, offering the bag around.

'Where shall I drop you?' Billy asked Rajiv.

'We'll start at the market.' Rajiv replied.

'I will drop you at the temple, then,' said Billy. 'The road into the market is impossible to drive along at this time of day because there is so much traffic.'

The temple was a tall building with elaborately carved pillars. A row of stone steps led up to a pair of huge wooden doors painted gold and covered with ornate carvings.

'Thanks,' said Rajiv. 'Where shall we meet you tonight?'

'Same place,' suggested Billy. 'Whoever gets here first can wait for the other, about five o'clock?'

'See you later,' Mandy called. Billy waved, pulled out and the jeep was swallowed back into the traffic. They crossed the road at traffic lights and headed towards the market.

'If we get separated we'll meet at the entrance,' yelled Rajiv above the noise of Indian music. The crowd was pushing them along and Mandy barely managed to stop herself being carried straight through the doorway and into the market itself.

'Phew!' James had almost lost his cap in the crowd and now stuffed it deep into his pocket. 'So many people. No wonder Billy prefers the park.'

'Now, to work,' Rajiv said. 'The best place to begin is the market itself. I can tell my friends what we are looking for and they can help. This way . . .'

Inside, the market was a hive of activity. Mandy and James were dazzled by the fruits and vegetables, many they had never seen before. Rajiv hurried them on past stalls selling roll upon roll of brilliantly coloured materials and brocades used for making the saris that most of the women wore. After this came spice and herb stalls that filled the air with exotic smells. But soon Mandy became aware of another smell.

'This part of the market is not a pleasant sight to see,' Rajiv said. 'But we must look.' Rajiv led them into an area full of animals in cages, all for sale. Some were so small that Mandy couldn't even see what was inside. Lining the walls were hundreds of songbirds in wicker cages, all vainly fluttering their wings against their prisons.

'But this is wildlife!' Mandy exclaimed, horrified. 'People shouldn't be allowed to sell wildlife.'

'This is India, Mandy. It happens,' Rajiv replied. 'It's not as bad as it used to be. More people nowadays would rather see the animals free than in cages. But it will take a long while until it is stopped.' Rajiv was scanning the crowded market. 'See that man over there?' he asked.

The man Rajiv pointed to was guiding a lorry that was backing up into the marketplace. 'That's one of the Banargee brothers, who deal in wild animals. The other one is probably driving.' The lorry stopped and the driver got out. He was dressed like his brother, in a dirty white shirt and dark trousers, but one arm was heavily bandaged.

'I wonder what happened to him?' James asked.

'I hope something bit him!' Mandy said.

'Now we know they are both here, we can start checking their places. We can leave the market by a back way. Let's go!' Rajiv ordered, hurrying them between the stalls.

Mandy didn't realise how horrible the smell had been until she was out in the fresh air. They passed a group of boys playing cricket with a flat piece of wood and a tennis ball. Rajiv greeted them all by name. There were nine of them ranging in age from about six to fourteen, Mandy guessed. All wore shorts; some had vests on and most were barefoot.

'I need a favour, my friends,' Rajiv. 'We are checking out the Banargee brothers' places . . . looking for tigers.'

The smaller boys' eyes widened.

'We have only one day to look so we need some help,' Rajiv continued.

'Tell us where to check, Raj,' said one of the bigger boys who wore just a pair of khaki shorts.

'OK, Mohan. If you all could check out the smaller lock-ups on Gandhi Road and the garages on Old Temple Road. Leave a mark for me. And if you,' Rajiv turned to the smaller boys, 'could keep an eye on the brothers. Listen out for anything they say. If they leave the market run ahead and warn us.' The little boys nodded and the older boys slapped hands with Rajiv. 'We can meet back here this afternoon, about two. Mandy, James and I will check their warehouses. Remember, we're looking for anywhere that could be used to hide a tiger,' he glanced at Mandy and James, before adding, 'dead or alive.'

'How will those little boys be able to warn us if the brothers are coming?' James was almost running to keep up with Rajiv who had set off at a cracking pace. 'They'll never be able to keep up.'

'You forget, James, they know this town. They can run through the alleys, climb over walls, even go underground in places for short cuts.' Rajiv stopped outside a very run-down, single-storey building. He peered through a filthy window at the side. 'This is one of their lock-ups, but it's full of stuff. It doesn't seem to have been used for a while.' He took a piece of a broken *chatti* from his pocket and drew an R near the window with it. It worked just like chalk. 'My friends will know it's been checked now.'

Rajiv led them up narrow winding alleys and down busy bustling streets, stopping at various warehouses and lock-ups on the way. As they criss-crossed the town they came across buildings with letters marked by *chatti* on them already, and Rajiv knew exactly who had been there. By two o'clock they had searched all the brothers' places but found nothing.

Mandy and James were tired and disappointed by the time they got back to the market. The others were already there and shook their heads.

'Nothing!' they reported.

'Maybe I'm wrong,' Mandy said miserably. 'I was sure we'd find something that would lead us to Sasha.'

'We've still got a few hours, Mandy.' James tried to sound optimistic. 'But we do seem to have looked absolutely everywhere. We can't have missed anywhere, can we, Rajiv?'

'Every place connected with those two has been checked,' Rajiv confirmed. He too looked disappointed. He waved to a man who rode towards them on a bicycle with a little freezer on the front full of ice-lollies. Then suddenly, he jumped up and stopped the man. They talked in Hindi for a while.

Rajiv came away smiling. 'This man's brother works for a man who sells property. He says that the Banargee brothers have rented a big warehouse on the Bypass Road. And,' he hesitated, 'they paid cash. It looks as if they want as few people as possible to know they have got the warehouse. We can check it this afternoon.'

Mandy's spirits shot up. 'It's not over yet, then. We might still find Sasha.'

The freezer full of lollies looked very tempting and she and James worked out that they had more than enough rupees to buy everyone a lolly before setting off on their last hope of finding Sasha.

The Bypass Road was lined with factories and warehouses, garages and workshops. Underneath railway arches men were selling all sorts of machinery, from bits of old cars to spare parts for tractors. Only when they reached the Banargees' warehouse did they realise their mistake. They hadn't kept a check on the Banargee brothers' whereabouts this time. The doors of the warehouse were open, and the lorry was parked outside.

Mandy knew they shouldn't confront the men – it would be too dangerous. But they had to look inside.

'Can we get round the back?' she whispered.

Rajiv led them down an alley that ran behind

the row of buildings to a gate at the back of the warehouse. Mandy tried it. It opened enough for them to squeeze inside. A metal ladder fixed to the wall led up to the warehouse roof.

'We can climb up and if there is a skylight we'll be able to see inside.' Rajiv was halfway up when he looked down at Mandy. 'Do you want to wait there?'

She took a deep breath. 'No, I have to see for myself if Sasha's there.' She took hold of the ladder and began to climb. Rather reluctantly, James followed.

They were in luck – the roof was made of corrugated iron and there was a skylight propped open with a plank of wood. Hardly daring to breathe they crept forward silently, lay on the roof and looked down into the building. Mandy's heart thudded. There was a lorry with covered-in sides and next to it what looked like a big box covered by a tarpaulin.

She nudged James and Rajiv and mouthed the word 'cage' at them. James nodded, but Rajiv was watching something else. Only then did Mandy take notice of the three men in the doorway. She drew a sharp breath. Two of them were the Banargee brothers; she recognised them from that morning. But it was the third man who surprised her. It was Sunnil, Rajiv's uncle.

Seven

'Let me ask Uncle Sunnil first,' Rajiv said. 'There may be a simple explanation. Nothing to do with tigers at all.'

They were walking back to the market to meet Billy. Mandy was sure that the cage covered by the tarpaulin contained the tigress, Sasha. She was all for getting Billy to go and look, before the brothers drove the lorry somewhere else and they lost their chance. But Rajiv had helped them so much and he loved tigers as much as she did. She had to listen to him.

'Even if we did want to go and look, the

Banargee brothers don't have to let us in. Let me ask my uncle what he was doing there,' Rajiv persuaded. 'He will have to tell me when he knows we saw him.'

'He's got a point, Mandy. We can't force our way in,' James pointed out. 'I expect there's a law about that, like at home.'

'OK, I suppose you're right,' Mandy said reluctantly. 'But we must do something about what we've seen soon,' she insisted. 'Before it's too late for Sasha!'

They decided not to say too much to Billy until Rajiv had spoken to Sunnie. When they reached the temple, Billy was waiting, and he looked worried.

'So, how did you get on? Did you find anything?' Billy asked.

'We searched everywhere, but we didn't find anything positive,' James replied, hesitantly.

'One place looked possible, but we couldn't get inside,' finished Mandy. Rajiv shot her a grateful look.

'How did you get on?' Mandy got the feeling things had not gone well for Billy.

'Not good, Mandy. The travel people I went

to see cannot find enough tourists to visit the park. They all want to go to the parks that have more facilities than we do. It's a problem.'

They were all lost in their own thoughts on the drive back to the park.

Back at Lookout Lodge, Mandy told her parents about their day. 'I'm sure there was a cage under the tarpaulin,' she insisted.

'But Rajiv and James are right, love,' said Adam Hope. 'You can't go breaking into places. Wait until we hear what Sunnil has to say. There may be a simple explanation.'

'I bet it's something to do with tigers.' Mandy wouldn't give in.

'Which reminds me,' Emily Hope said, tactfully changing the subject, 'Chhota is showing enormous improvement! Come and look at him.'

They trooped over to the hospital block. Chhota was pacing up and down in his cage, looking stronger and more solid than he'd looked even the day before.

'That's brilliant,' Mandy said. 'He looks like a proper tiger now, not a sickly little thing.'

She took a piece of meat, put it on a stick and pushed it through the bars. In a flash Chhota trapped it with his paw, lowered his body and, still watching Mandy, swallowed it down.

'A true success story, Mandy.' Billy came out of his office carrying his binoculars and a sweater.

Mandy was pleased to see that Billy seemed back to his old self. 'When can he be released?' she asked him.

'In a few days, when he's put on some more weight,' Billy replied. 'We can take him back to the den and then, off he goes. Do you agree, Emily? He's your patient after all.'

'That's fine,' Emily confirmed. 'He needs a final check-up but he's obviously doing very well.'

'I will see you all in the morning,' Billy announced. 'Roshan is dropping me at the hide. I need a night in the wild to clear my head.'

Mandy was delighted that Chhota had recovered so well but when she went to bed that night she couldn't sleep. She was troubled, too. Things didn't look good for the park. No tourists meant no income. Rajiv had said that they had only just enough money to keep Roshan on. If he had to find work elsewhere, how would Billy cope on his own? The villagers would bring their animals in and the poachers would have a free hand. As she drifted to sleep, she thought she heard a tiger roar, out in the jungle . . .

'Mandy, James, it's Rajiv. I have news for you!'

Mandy's eyes shot open. 'Rajiv!' She leaped out of bed, flung on some clothes and almost collided with James as they rushed out on to the veranda, where Rajiv and Roshan stood, waiting for them.

'You were right, Mandy,' Rajiv said, gravely. 'Uncle Sunnil broke down when Dad confronted him: the Banargee brothers do have a tiger hidden. They offered him money to help them catch it, and he took the money to buy my aunt the medicine she needs. He went there today to say he wanted nothing more to do with the poaching, but they say they will kill him if he pulls out. I wanted him to go to the police but he is too frightened.' Rajiv took a breath.

'The most important thing, though, is that he believes that the tiger is still alive.'

Mandy sighed in relief. 'What are they planning to do with the tiger? Do you think it could be Sasha?' Her head was now spinning with questions.

Roshan answered. 'Sunnil says they are taking live tigers up to the border with China and smuggling them across. Even if the border police find out, they silence them with bribes. The Banargee brothers are in charge of the poaching. They have been sneaking into the park to set snares. When a tiger is caught in the snare, they tranquillise it using a dart gun, get it out of the park and keep it tied up and semi-drugged in a cage till they're ready to move.'

'Do you know when that is?' James asked.

'They are planning to move soon,' Roshan replied.

'They are waiting to collect another tiger first.' Rajiv added.

'What's going on?' Adam and Emily Hope came out of their room, looking concerned. Anji and Sharma joined them.

Mandy quickly filled the new arrivals in on the devastating news.

'I will radio Billy,' said Roshan. 'He's got a handset with him at the hide. Maybe we can catch these poachers and put them behind bars.'

At that moment there was a tremendous crash from the hospital block.

'That sounded like Chhota's cage falling over,' Emily Hope said. They raced over to the hospital. Emily found the key, and opened the door. She was almost knocked off her feet as Chhota flew through the doorway like quicksilver and disappeared down the track. Inside the hospital they could see what had happened. Chhota had managed to overturn the cage and the spring release lock had triggered open.

Roshan took command. 'Rajiv, go get Yasmin. You can track Chhota. I will radio Billy. *Why* did he have to choose *this* night to stay in the hide?'

Rajiv ran and Roshan went into the radio room. He came back out a few minutes later with a gun and a box of cartridges. 'If the poachers are out tonight, Chhota is in danger. I've spoken to Billy,' he said, turning to Emily and Adam Hope. 'I will drive to the hide to collect him. But meanwhile, he agreed that Rajiv should track Chhota on Yasmin.'

'Adam and I will come with you,' said Mrs Hope, looking at her husband. Adam Hope nodded.

Rajiv arrived with Yasmin. Mandy and James looked at Mr and Mrs Hope.

'What about us?' Mandy asked.

'You two go with Rajiv,' Adam Hope said. 'I know there's no way you two intend to stay behind!'

The elephant knelt and Mandy and James climbed up.

Although it was too dark to see much, Rajiv was able to follow the tiger cub's movements by the alarm cries of the other animals. Langur monkeys coughed when Chhota was near. He was too young a tiger to be completely stealthy and he occasionally broke twigs and crashed through the undergrowth. Sambar and chital deer barked alarm calls as he passed and peacocks roosting in the trees gave haunting shrieks.

Yasmin trod confidently after the tiger cub, who seemed to be wandering aimlessly through the forest without a place to head for.

'He is not visiting any of the dens. I don't know where he is going,' Rajiv said, puzzled. 'This part of the park is very remote, I have only been here a couple of times in the jeep.' They followed Chhota's trail for hours. Then, as dawn began to break over the forest, Yasmin suddenly halted. Rajiv tapped her head with his stick, and clicked to her but she would not move forward. Instead she backed up and moved around a clump of bamboo.

'Yasmin seems to sense that there is now another tiger near,' Rajiv said in a worried voice. 'It could be that Chhota has been following the scent of another tiger,' he explained. 'I hope it isn't Zemo. He'd make short work of Chhota.'

'Would he do that?' Mandy asked, alarmed for Chhota.

Rajiv tapped Yasmin to encourage her to move on. 'Let's hope not,' he said, quietly.

Yasmin continued slowly on, the way

becoming more and more difficult for her as the undergrowth thickened. And then, to Mandy, James and Rajiv's relief, the track opened up again.

But a terrible sight greeted them. Up ahead, sprawled across the track lay a tiger. One foot was swollen and bloody and caught fast in a wire snare.

'It's Tara,' Rajiv declared grimly. 'See the mark on the side of her head like a catapult? I'd know her anywhere.'

Rajiv climbed down and tethered Yasmin to a nearby tree. 'James, call Billy on the radio handset and tell him we are at the south side of the park,' he instructed. 'Tell him it's the animal trail under the banyan trees. He will know it. He knows every part of the park.'

James pressed the transmit button. Nothing happened.

'Try it again,' Mandy urged.

'There are too many trees, the signal is breaking up.' Rajiv said. 'Call base. Mum will hear it and pass on the message.'

James tried again and this time a crackling reply came from Anji. He gave her the information then switched off the handset to conserve the batteries.

Mandy began to climb down from Yasmin, but Rajiv warned her and James to stay close to the elephant. 'That way a tiger will see you as being part of Yasmin, and you will be safe.'

'Do you think Tara is still alive?' Mandy asked, shakily. The tiger was so still.

Rajiv stood watching the tiger for several seconds. 'I think I can just see her breathing,' he replied.

'Then there's a chance we can save her!' Mandy exclaimed. 'But she needs help immediately. That snare is like a tourniquet. It's cutting off the blood supply. She could lose her leg! Let me try!' Mandy stepped forward.

But Rajiv held her back. 'No, Mandy, it's too risky,' he said. 'I insist that you and James stay close to Yasmin.'

Mandy looked at James then nodded reluctantly.

Rajiv started to move forward towards Tara, then stopped as a low warning growl sounded out. 'Another tiger,' he warned softly.

Then, out of the undergrowth stepped

Chhota. He stood over his mother and snarled at Rajiv.

'Chhota!' cried Mandy, before she could stop herself. Though Chhota didn't take his eyes off Rajiv, he stopped snarling.

Rajiv slowly and carefully made his way back to the others, and sighed. 'Now we must wait for the others to arrive. Though Chhota seems to have recognised us, he might attack if he sees us as a threat to his mother. We will have to tranquillise him in order to get to Tara.'

They stood waiting, anxious and frustrated by their inability to help. At last they heard the sound of a vehicle approaching.

'Thank goodness!' Mandy exclaimed. Now they could get both the tigers safely back to the hospital and treated.

'But that's not one of the Lodge jeeps,' said Rajiv tensely. 'The sound of the engine is different.'

They all looked at each other, thinking the same thing. The poachers had arrived!

Eight

Suddenly Chhota roared, his head turning this way and that as if he wasn't sure where to watch. The vehicle pulled into view. It was the lorry they had seen at the warehouse.

'Quick!' said Rajiv urgently. He untethered Yasmin and guided her back into the undergrowth.

They watched two men emerge from the lorry. The Banargee brothers. One carried a gun; the other had a bandaged arm and held what looked like a big sack.

As the men edged forwards towards Tara,

Chhota turned and snarled at them.

'Two instead of one,' said the man with the sack. 'But we don't have enough tranquilliser with us to dope the little one as well.'

Horrified, Mandy, James and Rajiv watched as the man with the gun raised the barrel and pointed it at Chhota. 'Then we must do it this way instead,' he said coldly.

'Don't you dare!' Mandy shouted. Before anyone could stop her Mandy ran out on to the track. 'Stop! Don't you dare shoot him!'

Startled, the poacher swung the gun from Chhota to Mandy.

'Get away, silly girl. You think you can stop me?' he sneered.

'Yes, we will!' By now, James and Rajiv had stepped forward too. The men began to look panicked.

'We know who you are!' Mandy was desperately trying to stall for time. 'We've radioed for help and the police are on their way. They'll be here any minute.'

The man with the gun looked desperate. Chhota still stood by his mother. The poacher curled his finger around the trigger and took aim again.

Suddenly there was a terrifying rushing and tearing from the undergrowth. Before anyone could move, another tiger came bounding out from the bushes down the track. In one mighty leap it sprang on to the man. There was a boom as the gun went off then a crash as man and tiger hit the ground.

For a second there was a stunned silence and nobody moved. Then the other poacher turned and ran to their lorry. With blood streaming from a head wound the man with the gun scrambled to his feet and staggered off behind him. The lorry screeched away.

'Bada!' Rajiv cried, running over to where the tiger lay. 'It's Bada and he's dead.'

Mandy was desolate. Chhota was alive but his brother was dead. Hot salty tears slid down her face. 'Bada saved him,' she said through her tears. 'He sacrificed himself to save Chhota and their mother.' Then Mandy remembered. 'I thought I heard a tiger calling to Chhota last night, as I fell asleep,' she said.

'It must have been Bada calling him to their

mother,' James said, taking off his glasses and rubbing his eyes. Rajiv buried his face in Bada's coat. They were all heartbroken.

'Poor Bada,' James said. 'He must have wanted his brother with him for comfort.'

'Where is Chhota?' Mandy said. She looked around frantically, but the cub had gone.

'He will have run away, Mandy,' Rajiv replied. 'The noise of the gunshot must have terrified him.'

Rajiv went a little closer to Tara. 'She's still alive,' he said, his voice urgent. 'We may still be able to save her, if the jeep arrives soon.'

Soon afterwards the sound of the jeep's engine could be heard, straining through the undergrowth. 'At last!' Mandy exclaimed.

While Adam and Emily Hope immediately set to work removing the trap from Tara's leg, Mandy, James and Rajiv told the others the shocking details of what had just happened.

'Who knows what these men are capable of?' said Emily Hope, shaking her head. 'Brave little Bada probably saved you all.'

'What about the lorry, and the other tiger?' said Mandy, remembering that the poachers planned to move soon.

'The most important thing now,' said her father, 'is to get Tara back to camp.'

Roshan, Billy, Adam Hope and Rajiv carried Tara over to the jeep, while Mandy, James and Emily Hope brought up the rear, carrying Bada's body. The jeep was parked not far from where Yasmin was waiting patiently.

The jeep set off back to camp.

Mandy and James helped Rajiv to wrap Bada's body in a blanket and load it on to Yasmin's back. 'I will bury Bada under the bean tree by the river,' Rajiv said. 'And when the flowers come each year, it will always remind me of him.'

The jeep arrived back at camp first. By the time Yasmin deposited Mandy and James at the mounting steps, Tara was on the operating table.

Billy was waiting for them. 'Roshan has told me all about Sunnil and the Banargee brothers. I suggest we go and take a look. I think we have more than enough evidence to force an entry into that warehouse.'

Roshan took over Yasmin so that Rajiv could also go with Billy.

Billy started the jeep. 'Rajiv, you sit in the front and direct me. Mandy and James, jump in the back.'

'Suppose we're too late?' worried Mandy.

'Then we'll follow them up to the border if necessary,' said Billy.

They sped through the valley to Kasatni but when they arrived the warehouse was all locked up. Billy hammered on the doors with his fists. The owner of the garage next door came out to see what all the noise was.

'You're too late, they have gone,' he said.

'When? How long ago?' Billy demanded. 'Which way did they go?'

'Not fifteen minutes since,' the garage owner said. 'Headed north. They came to me for some petrol but I am waiting for a delivery myself.'

Billy looked at his watch. It was just before nine. 'There is only one road they can take to the north from here. If they have to buy petrol first there's a chance we can get on the road before them and block it. Let's go!'

Mandy and James clung on tight, the jeep bouncing up and down through the potholes. James ducked to avoid hitting his head on the roof. Billy forced his way through the traffic and out of town. Mandy almost fell out of her seat as Billy took a corner at speed.

'Don't worry in the back. I am a safe driver.' Billy slammed on the brakes at a red light and they all lurched forward.

Billy pushed the jeep as fast as it would go. James heard a siren and looked back. 'Oh no! We're being followed by the police.'

But Billy didn't slow down. 'If the police follow us to the poachers, so much the better!' he said.

At last they reached a crossroad and Billy turned right. He had gone only a few metres when the police car caught up. It pulled in front of them, forcing him to stop. Two angry policemen leaped out and yanked open Billy's door. One of them started to shout at Billy in Hindi.

Wearily Billy started to explain. Rajiv turned to the back seat, translating for Mandy and James what was being said.

Then one of the policemen turned to them and said in English, 'What is the poacher's vehicle like?'

'I can tell you that,' Mandy ventured. 'It's dark green, and the sides are made of brown material.' She tried to remember some more. 'Oh yes, there's a big scratch on the tailgate.'

The policemen looked at each other.

'I am afraid you are too late,' one of them said. 'That lorry passed by already. I know because I stopped them for speeding too.'

Mandy couldn't bear the thought that they might get away. 'Can't you help us? Please? If we can catch them we can save the tiger. She has three little cubs that need her desperately.'

The policemen made a decision. 'Follow us!' They jumped in their car and put the flashing light on.

Billy followed behind, the jeep going all-out to keep up the pace.

'There's the lorry!' Rajiv cried.

'And it's stopped.' James added.

As they drew near they saw that the lorry was surrounded by hundreds of goats, completely blocking the road. The Banargee brothers were waving their fists in the air but the lorry wasn't going anywhere.

The police car screeched to a halt and

Billy pulled up behind them.

'It's Uncle Sunnil!' Rajiv jumped out and ran over to the man who had herded the goats on to the road.

'Let's look in the lorry,' Mandy urged. She could hardly bear to see what was inside.

Suppose it wasn't Sasha? Or worse still, what if, after all this, the tigress was already dead?'

The policemen drew back the curtain.

'It's Sasha,' Billy exclaimed. 'My poor, poor Sasha.' The tigress, heavily drugged, had been laid spread-eagled on her front and each leg tied to a corner of the cage. 'I must get her back to the park immediately.'

'I am so sorry,' Sunnil said, coming up to them. 'I felt so bad about what I had done, I wanted to help. I left last night and walked the goats to the road, then waited here in the field until the lorry came, then I led the goats out,' he explained.

Billy patted him on the shoulder. 'But you have done well, now, my friend. Thank you.'

'What about the jeep?' James asked. 'If you take the lorry, there's nobody to drive it back.'

'If Rajiv will lead the goats back to the village,

I can drive it back,' Sunnil offered.

'We'll come with you, Rajiv, shall we, James?' Mandy said. James nodded.

'Wait for us at the village please, Uncle. You can drive us to the park,' Rajiv said.

'I will wait outside the old school.' Sunnil turned the jeep round and, with the lorry following, drove back down the road.

The Banargee brothers were safely hand-cuffed together in the police car.

'It will be prison for them,' said the policeman as he got in the car, 'for a long, long time!'

Later that day, when they were all back at camp, Mrs Hope declared Sasha very traumatised, but uninjured. And now that the poachers were locked up, everyone felt a lot more relaxed.

Sunnil stood before them, his head bowed. 'I am sorry I have been so foolish. I am glad that the tigers will be all right and I will never do such a thing again. If you wish it, I will leave the village.' He looked at Billy.

'No,' said Billy resignedly. 'What you did was wrong but if it hadn't been for your actions at the end we may have lost Sasha for ever.' Billy was silent for a moment. 'I just wish we could find a solution to the problem. If only the park could afford to provide some work for the village, but without the tourists visiting, funds will be short.'

'Well, I have an idea,' Mandy ventured, looking at her mum and dad for support.

'Go on,' Emily urged.

'Is that old school used any more?' Mandy asked.

'No. People are moving away from the village. There isn't any work,' said Sunnil. 'It is one of the reasons that the village is dying.'

'Then why don't you turn the old school into a lodge for tourists? If the village offered accommodation, you could attract more tourists to the park. Some of the villagers – like Rajiv's aunt and Sunnil, for instance – could run it and get some money, and the park would be better off, too.'

Billy looked thoughtful.

'My wife is getting better now. I think she would be very keen,' said Sunnil. He was getting enthusiastic now.

'And if we have a lot more tourists,' Billy

reasoned, 'I would need a driver to bring them in and out.'

'Uncle Sunnil could do that job, too,' Rajiv suggested shyly.

'Indeed he could,' Billy agreed.

'We will start today,' Sunnil said. 'I will go and tell others in the village.'

After a few days, Sasha slowly returned to normal. Her milk had come back, and Billy planned to put the cubs in with her.

'No more bottles for you now,' said Mandy sadly, as she cuddled her cub for the last time.

'Did you know that every single tiger's stripes are unique, Mandy?' Billy asked quietly. 'Would you know your cub again?'

'Would I! I know every one of his stripes by heart now.'

'Then in years to come you may visit here again and recognise your tiger. You will be able to say, "That tiger there is *my* tiger!" and you will be right,' Billy smiled.

Mandy smiled back and sighed in contentment. Between them they had saved three tiger cubs and their mother – not to mention Chhota and his mother, Tara. Mandy's smile faded as Bada came into her mind. Poor, brave Bada. But, all in all, together they had done something good for tiger conservation.

'It's time now, Mandy, James, Sharma.' Billy put his arms round them and shepherded them out to Sasha's cage.

Mandy buried her face in her cub's fur. 'Goodbye. Have a good life,' she whispered. 'Grow up big and strong. You take care and learn from your mother.' The cub licked the tear that was sliding down her cheek. 'One day I'll come back and we'll recognise each other again.'

'Off you go.' They watched Billy put the cubs into the big cage with their mother. The cubs went wild, rubbing themselves affectionately against her fur and mewing happily. Minutes later they were suckling contentedly.

'Well, Mandy, are you happy to see them back with their mother?' Billy asked.

'I am,' she said slowly, 'but there's just one thing.'

'And what is that?'

'I was just thinking about Bada. When the

new lodge for the tourists is finished, could you call it "Bada Lodge"?'

'That's an excellent idea, Mandy. I'll be proud to call it that,' Billy agreed.

Three days later, Emily Hope declared that Tara's foot had healed enough for her to be released. 'She will always have a callus on it, but Billy is sure it won't impair her hunting ability.'

At dawn the following day Billy, Adam Hope and Roshan took the jeep with Tara's cage on a trailer. Mandy, James and Mrs Hope went on Yasmin with Rajiv.

'Wait, wait.' Anji and Sharma came running across the compound. 'Have you got room for us too?'

It was a squash in the *howdah* but they were all too excited to worry. When they got to Tara's den it was empty and quiet. Mandy had secretly hoped Chhota would be there. He hadn't been seen since Bada was shot.

Rajiv stopped Yasmin a short distance from the den. Billy backed the jeep up so the trailer was as near to the den as possible. When he pulled the rope to lift the door of the cage, Tara made no attempt to go out.

'Come on, girl,' Emily Hope muttered. 'You'll be fine.'

They waited for an age. And then Mandy gasped. 'Look, on the ledge. It's Chhota.'

Chhota gave a grumbly roar and jumped down from the ledge. Mandy could see how much stronger he had become. Tara sprang out of the cage and was beside her cub in the blink of an eye. Tara licked Chhota's face and led him away towards the den. Chhota stopped for a moment and looked back at Mandy. 'Go!' she whispered. And Chhota turned and padded after his mother.

ANIMAL ARK

Lucy Daniels

1	KITTENS IN THE KITCHEN	£3.99	❏
2	PONY IN THE PORCH	£3.99	❏
3	PUPPIES IN THE PANTRY	£3.99	❏
4	GOAT IN THE GARDEN	£3.99	❏
5	HEDGEHOGS IN THE HALL	£3.99	❏
6	BADGER IN THE BASEMENT	£3.99	❏
7	CUB IN THE CUPBOARD	£3.99	❏
8	PIGLET IN A PLAYPEN	£3.99	❏
9	OWL IN THE OFFICE	£3.99	❏
10	LAMB IN THE LAUNDRY	£3.99	❏
11	BUNNIES IN THE BATHROOM	£3.99	❏
12	DONKEY ON THE DOORSTEP	£3.99	❏
13	HAMSTER IN A HAMPER	£3.99	❏
14	GOOSE ON THE LOOSE	£3.99	❏
15	CALF IN THE COTTAGE	£3.99	❏
16	KOALA IN A CRISIS	£3.99	❏
17	WOMBAT IN THE WILD	£3.99	❏
18	ROO ON THE ROCK	£3.99	❏
19	SQUIRRELS IN THE SCHOOL	£3.99	❏
20	GUINEA-PIG IN THE GARAGE	£3.99	❏
21	FAWN IN THE FOREST	£3.99	❏
22	SHETLAND IN THE SHED	£3.99	❏
23	SWAN IN THE SWIM	£3.99	❏
24	LION BY THE LAKE	£3.99	❏
25	ELEPHANTS IN THE EAST	£3.99	❏
26	MONKEYS ON THE MOUNTAIN	£3.99	❏
27	DOG AT THE DOOR	£3.99	❏
28	FOALS IN THE FIELD	£3.99	❏
29	SHEEP AT THE SHOW	£3.99	❏
30	RACOONS ON THE ROOF	£3.99	❏
31	DOLPHIN IN THE DEEP	£3.99	❏
32	BEARS IN THE BARN	£3.99	❏
33	OTTER IN THE OUTHOUSE	£3.99	❏
34	WHALE IN THE WAVES	£3.99	❏
35	HOUND AT THE HOSPITAL	£3.99	❏
36	RABBITS ON THE RUN	£3.99	❏
37	HORSE IN THE HOUSE	£3.99	❏
38	PANDA IN THE PARK	£3.99	❏
	SHEEPDOG IN THE SNOW	£3.99	❏
	KITTEN IN THE COLD	£3.99	❏
	FOX IN THE FROST	£3.99	❏
	HAMSTER IN THE HOLLY	£3.99	❏
	PONIES AT THE POINT	£3.99	❏
	SEAL ON THE SHORE	£3.99	❏
	ANIMAL ARK FAVOURITES	£3.99	❏

All Hodder Children's books are available at your local bookshop, or can be ordered direct from the publisher. Just tick the titles you would like and complete the details below. Prices and availability are subject to change without prior notice.

Please enclose a cheque or postal order made payable to *Bookpoint Ltd*, and send to: Hodder Children's Books, 39 Milton Park, Abingdon, OXON OX14 4TD, UK. Email Address: orders@bookpoint.co.uk

If you would prefer to pay by credit card, our call centre team would be delighted to take your order by telephone. Our direct line *01235 400414* (lines open 9.00 am–6.00 pm Monday to Saturday, 24 hour message answering service). Alternatively you can send a fax on *01235 400454*.

TITLE	FIRST NAME	SURNAME

ADDRESS

DAYTIME TEL:	POST CODE

If you would prefer to pay by credit card, please complete:
Please debit my Visa/Access/Diner's Card/American Express (delete as applicable) card no:

Signature ....

Expiry Date: ....

If you would NOT like to receive further information on our products please tick the box. ☐